**'It's been a lo...
I've enjoyed it ... ...ank
you.'**

'I've enjoyed it too,' she said.

He caught the scent of her perfume, completely in keeping with that exotic aura about her that he had noticed at their very first meeting, and as he stood looking down at her, and her eyes met his, it seemed that all the events of that quite extraordinary day reached a peak and culminated in a moment of totally unexpected magic between them.

It was without the slightest hesitation that he bent his head. It seemed the most natural thing in the world for his lips to meet hers in a kiss that somehow seemed to make time stand still. Her mouth beneath his felt soft, tasted sweet, but even as he felt an uncontrollable leap of desire that sent his senses spinning into oblivion it was over, and she was drawing away.

He stared at her. What in the world had he done?

Laura MacDonald was born and bred in the Isle of Wight, where she still lives with her husband. The Island is a place of great natural beauty, and forms the backdrop for many of Laura's books. She has been writing fiction since she was a child. Her first book was published in the 1980s, and she has been writing full time since 1991, during which time she has produced over forty books for both adults and children. When she isn't writing her hobbies include painting, reading and researching family history.

Recent titles by the same author:

THE SURGEON'S PREGNANCY SURPRISE
THE DOCTOR'S SECRET SON
THE LATIN SURGEON (*Mediterranean Doctors*)
THE POLICE DOCTOR'S DISCOVERY
  (*Police Surgeons*)

THE DOCTORS'
NEW-FOUND
FAMILY

BY
LAURA MACDONALD

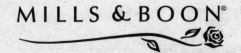

First published in Great Britain 2006
Harlequin Mills & Boon Limited,
Eton House, 18-24 Paradise Road, Richmond, Surrey TW9 1SR

© Laura MacDonald 2006

ISBN-13: 978 0 263 84761 1
ISBN-10:   0 263 84761 6

Set in Times Roman 10½ on 12¾ pt
03-1006-50284

Printed and bound in Spain
by Litografia Rosés, S.A., Barcelona

THE DOCTORS' NEW-FOUND FAMILY

CHAPTER ONE

'HI, DAD.'

'Hello, Jamie! This is a nice surprise. I wasn't expecting to hear from you today.'

'Can you talk? You're not cutting up somebody's heart, are you?'

Nathan smiled and transferred his mobile phone to his other ear. 'Yes, I can talk and, no, I'm not cutting up somebody's heart, as you put it.'

'Joshua Bartrum didn't believe me when I said my dad was a heart surgeon.'

'So who's Joshua Bartrum?' Nathan felt a stab of pain as yet again he realised how little he knew about his son's day-to-day life.

'He's a boy at my school,' Jamie replied. 'He said his dad was a brain surgeon.'

'And is he?' asked Nathan.

'No, Mum said he was a taxi-driver.' There was a pause. 'I wish you were a taxi-driver, Dad,' he said.

Another stab. 'Do you? Why's that?'

'Because it's cool and…because Joshua Bartrum sees his dad all the time…' Another pause during which Nathan struggled to find the right thing to say. 'Did you know,' Jamie went on after a moment, 'next Sunday is Father's Day…?'

'Is that so?'

'Mum and Martin are going to London for the weekend and I was wondering if I could come with them and stay with you…or will you be working?'

'I'm not sure, Jamie, but I tell you what, I'll check up and if I'm not on call, it would be wonderful.'

'Cool!' There was no disguising the excitement in the boy's voice.

'How is your mum, Jamie?' asked Nathan.

'She's OK.' There was a brief silence. 'Dad,' he said, 'where are you?'

'At this very moment?' He lifted his head and looked around. 'I'm sitting at the top of a flight of steps which leads from the terrace of a big house into beautiful gardens that run right down to the river Thames.'

'What are you doing there?'

'I'm at a party at the home of some friends of mine—Mr and Mrs Lathwell-Foxe. Do you remember them, Jamie? Mr Lathwell-Foxe works at the hospital with me.'

'Yes, I think so,' Jamie replied. 'Do you like your new job, Dad?' he added, and his voice was wistful now.

'Yes, at least, I think I'm going to like it—I've only been there a few days.'

'I wish you weren't so far away.'

'I know, Jamie. But, hey, listen, London isn't that far from Chester, you know—not on the motorway…'

'No, I s'ppose… I'd better go now, Dad.'

'All right, son. I'll speak to you again soon about the weekend. Take care, lots of love…' Nathan's eyes were misty as he pressed the off button on his phone—conversations with his son always did that to him and he knew that would be especially so now since he'd moved even further away from the boy's home than when he had lived in Oxford.

Still sitting on the top of the flight of stone steps, something suddenly caught his attention, a flash of colour, and he glanced down just as a woman walked beneath an archway immediately below him and into the garden. Whether it was because his eyes were still misty from talking to Jamie or because they had spoken of Jamie's mother, he wasn't sure, but just for one moment there was something about the woman with her curtain of dark hair that brushed her shoulders that reminded him of Susan. Or maybe it was the tall slenderness of her body, or the way she moved, gracefully, one hand gently touching the heads of flowers as she passed the herbaceous borders, that stirred something in his memory. He couldn't see her face and probably she was nothing like Susan, but just for a moment his breath had caught in his throat as he was reminded of her, or at least of the way she had looked all those years ago when they had first met, when everything between them had been wonderful. But that had been then and this was now and he didn't want to think about Susan. Jamie, yes. Always. But not Susan.

Taking a deep breath, he stood up and slipped his mobile phone into his pocket. By this time the woman had disappeared and he turned and walked back the way he had come onto the terrace.

'Nathan! There you are.' His hostess, Claudia, had appeared in the open French doors that were thrown back to allow the cool evening breeze into the drawing room behind her. It had been a perfect June day and the home of the

Lathwell-Foxes, overlooking the Thames, an ideal setting for a drinks party. 'I wondered where you had got to.'

'I was admiring your lovely gardens,' he said.

'Thank you.' Claudia inclined her head and, taking his arm, led him into the drawing room. 'They are Rory's pride and joy—not that he has time to do too much himself these days. Most of his time seems to be spent at St Benedict's, which, no doubt, if you're not careful, will also become your fate,' she added darkly.

'I guess it goes with the territory,' he said.

'But do you think you're going to like it?' She leaned a little closer and he caught the scent of her perfume.

'You're the second person in the space of a few moments to ask me that,' he replied.

'Really?' She looked around a little vaguely and he knew she wondered to whom he had been talking in the garden when most of the guests seemed to still be in the drawing room, not yet having spilled out onto the terrace, which, no doubt, they would shortly be doing. Briefly, the thought of the dark-haired woman entered his mind then he dismissed it. 'I took a call on my mobile from Jamie,' he explained.

'Oh, yes,' she said quickly. 'Of course. How is he?'

'He's fine, wants to come down next weekend for Father's Day.'

'And will he be able to?'

'If St Benedict's allows it,' he replied.

At that moment Claudia's husband, Rory, appeared at her elbow and she turned to him. 'Nathan has just been talking to Jamie,' she said.

And how is Jamie?' asked Rory.

'He's well.' Nathan nodded.

'Well, maybe we'll get to see a bit more of him now you're in London.' Rory remarked.

'He's hoping to come down with his mother next weekend.'

'Ah, Susan.' Rory raised one eyebrow. 'How is she?'

'She's OK,' Nathan said, and took a drink from a tray carried by one of the catering staff that the Lathwell-Foxes had employed for the evening.

'Has she married the guy yet?'

'No, not yet, but I understand it's on the cards.' Nathan's jaw tightened. Out of the corner of his eye he noticed that the dark-haired woman he had seen in the garden had just come into the room. He had been quite right—face to face she was nothing like Susan.

'Well, let's hope she doesn't lead him such a merry dance as she led you,' said Rory.

'On the other hand, it could be argued it would be poetic justice if she does,' Claudia observed tartly. 'Maybe then he would understand there is a price to be paid for breaking up a marriage.'

'My marriage was on the skids long before he came along,' said Nathan quietly.

'Shall we change the subject?' asked Rory.

'Good idea,' Nathan agreed. Across the room he saw that the dark-haired woman had also taken a drink from the waitress and was looking around the room rather uncertainly, as if she was searching for someone to talk to.

'So how's your first week at St Benedict's been going?'

'Pretty good really.' Nathan took a sip of his drink. 'Richard Parker seems to run a good team on the cardiac unit.'

'Don't know a lot about him,' said Rory. 'Our paths don't cross that often, with me being over in Orthopaedics, but from what I've heard he's very highly thought of—you should do all right on his team.'

'Well, I'm grateful to you for pointing out the job in the first place,' said Nathan, then as Claudia drifted away to greet more guests, he saw that the dark-haired woman was talking to an older woman whom he recognised as an anaesthetist at the hospital.

'Don't mention it,' said Rory. 'It's great to have you aboard. I guess you don't know too many people yet. This could be a good opportunity…' He glanced around, his gaze falling upon the two woman standing in front of the drawing-room fire-place. 'You know Diana Fellows?'

'Yes, we met briefly—anaesthetist, isn't she?'

'Consultant anaesthetist, actually. Shortly coming up for retirement—very much one of the old school…'

'And the lady with her?' asked Nathan casually.

'Ah, the lovely Olivia—you haven't met her?'

'No, not yet.'

'Oh, we must remedy that.' Rory took off across the room, leaving Nathan no option but to follow him. He wasn't sure how he felt about meeting his mystery dark-haired lady. There had been something about her that had immediately attracted him, though whether it had been the resemblance to Susan or not he didn't know. What he did know was that he didn't really want to pursue anyone that would remind him of his ex-wife, however fleeting that resemblance might be, and that, really, the image of the woman as she had moved so gracefully through the garden should probably remain just that—a de-lightful and slightly mysterious image.

'Olivia.' Rory had reached her then turned towards him again. 'There's somebody I'd like you to meet. Nathan, this is Olivia Gilbert. Olivia is a paediatrician at St Benedict's. Olivia, this is Nathan Carrington—he's just joined us from St Anne's in Oxford. Nathan has joined Richard Parker's team as consultant cardiac surgeon.'

'Hello,' she said, and Nathan was aware of the cool touch of her fingers as she took his hand.

'Pleased to meet you,' he murmured, desperately hoping that his own hand wasn't hot and sweaty. Briefly he was aware of large hazel eyes with thick dark lashes, a flawless olive complexion and that glossy curtain of hair so dark it appeared almost black. He had difficulty gauging her age— it could have been anywhere from late twenties to late thirties—but while her whole demeanour had the freshness of youth about it, the grace of her movements and a certain sense of elegance suggested a touch of maturity which common sense told him must be the case for her to have attained the position of paediatrician.

'I saw you,' he said, 'just now in the garden.' Why on earth had he said that? It made him sound like a babbling schoolboy.

'Really?' she said. 'I was enjoying the flowers and the cool breeze.'

'It certainly has been hot today.' Mercifully Diana Fellows came to his rescue, preventing him from making yet another inane comment. 'Too damn hot as far as I'm concerned.' She gave a short laugh that sounded rather like a bark. 'So you're the new heart man.' Speculatively she eyed Nathan up and down then launched into an in-depth discussion on the rest of the cardiac team and their policies. To his dismay, he realised that Olivia was edging away and before he could do anything about extricating himself from Diana's clutches, she had joined another group who eventually drifted out onto the terrace.

By the time that Diana's attention had been taken by someone else and he was able to escape onto the coolness of the terrace, there was no sign of Olivia. Quite why he wanted to speak to her again he wasn't sure. He now knew it certainly had nothing to do with the fleeting resemblance to Susan because fleeting was all it had been and, as he had suspected, on closer acquaintance Olivia was nothing like Susan. But something certainly had attracted him.

He thought she'd gone, left the party, but later, when the soft June twilight was stealing up from the river and settling on the lawns, and the scent of Claudia's roses was at its height, he caught a glimpse of the lilac blue chiffon of the dress she was wearing and with a jolt realised that she was sitting alone at the far end of the terrace.

Olivia hadn't really wanted to go to the party, fond as she was of both Claudia and Rory. She tried to tell herself the reason for this reluctance was that it was Helene's day off and she felt like it was taking advantage of her to expect her to be around for the evening, but deep down she knew the real reason was because she still wasn't really into social gatherings of any kind. Which was crazy really, when she considered how much she had once adored the social scene, and it hadn't ended with attending social events. She, in turn, had loved entertaining, whether formal drinks parties like this one or dinner parties where she had prided herself on such attention to detail that every one of her guests' needs was catered for. There had been the winter weekend parties and dinners and with the onset of the warmer weather, the summer lunches, race meetings, barbeques and at least one midsummer ball.

Now, as she sat on the stone balustrade at one end of

Claudia's terrace in the gathering dusk, she found herself hard pushed to remember the last event she had attended. It must have been before...but then everything was before because very little had happened since.

'Hello again.'

She looked up sharply and found a man standing before her. 'Oh,' she said, 'you made me jump.'

'I'm sorry,' he said. 'I didn't mean to.'

'It's all right. I was miles away.' It was the man she'd met earlier, the one Rory had introduced as the new cardiac surgeon at St Benedict's. Tonight had been the first time she'd seen him as their paths hadn't yet crossed at work. He had seemed pleasant enough but, somewhat disturbingly, when she had first caught sight of him across the drawing room, it had fleetingly occurred to her that once, in what now seemed like another lifetime, he was the type of man she would have found attractive. Not now, of course. Any hint of that was right out of the question. But once, long ago, a man of over average height with dark hair and a rather dangerous glint in a pair of green eyes would have definitely appealed.

'Mind if I join you?' he asked, and not really waiting for a reply he sat down beside her on the edge of the balustrade. He was wearing a dark jacket and trousers and the white of his shirt seemed to glow in the half-light. She noticed he'd loosened his tie and undone the top two buttons of his shirt.

'The weather's been perfect,' he said, 'just right for a party like this.'

'Oh, Claudia orders it, along with the caterers,' she said. 'Didn't you know?'

He laughed, an easy laugh with an infectious note in it that made her join in. 'How long have you known Claudia...and

Rory?' he asked after a moment during which any tension or awkwardness there might have been between them seemed to dissolve in the balmy night air.

'Claudia and I go back a long way… We were at school together and Rory, well, we're both at St Benedict's, of course.' She paused and stole a sideways glance at him. His profile against the light from the drawing-room windows really was rather interesting. 'Is that how you met Rory?'

'Lord, no. A bit like you and Claudia, Rory and I go way back—we were at medical school together. In recent years we sort of lost touch for a while, you know how it is, but now, well…' He shrugged lightly, leaving the sentence unfinished. 'So.' He turned his head to look at her. 'What about you? How long have you been at St Benedict's?'

'For ever, really, or it seems like that. I did my training there,' she explained, 'and somehow, well, I just stayed…'

'And now you're a paediatrician? Sorry, I didn't mean that to sound patronising.' He paused. 'Was that always your long-term plan?'

'No.' She shook her head. 'I had originally decided on general practice but, I don't know, one thing seemed to lead to another and I found myself more and more involved with working with children and now I really wouldn't want to be doing anything else…' A shrill laugh from further along the terrace interrupted her and they both looked to see what was happening. A group of young people had just climbed up the steps from the garden onto the terrace and were heading for the French doors of the drawing room.

'They are rather late,' observed Nathan.

'They'll have arrived by boat,' said Olivia. 'That tall young man is Rory's junior houseman.'

'Not gate-crashers, then?' said Nathan with a smile.

'No, Rory would have made short shrift of them if they were.' She was silent again then, as the chatter of voices faded and quiet descended on the terrace once more, she said, 'What about you?'

'Me? I'm not a gate-crasher.' She sensed rather than saw his smile in the settling dusk.

'No,' she said, 'I know you're not. What I meant was, did you always want to specialise in heart surgery?'

'Actually, yes, believe it or not. I followed my father into the profession. It was simply always what I wanted to do.'

'Wonderful,' she said. 'When you have a dream and you're able to fulfil that dream.'

'Yes, I suppose so.'

'What brought you to St Benedict's?' Suddenly she was curious in spite of her self-imposed no-involvement rule.

'A chance meeting with Rory,' he said. 'He told me about the position that was becoming vacant. It was promotion for me and held much better prospects than my last position in Oxford so I decided to go for it.'

'Do you think you made the right decision?'

'I hope so. Actually, yes, I think I have, but of course time will tell. I haven't been there a week yet.'

'Well, I hope it will be right for you. Richard Parker is very well respected.' She took a deep breath. 'Actually,' she said, 'I'm going to have to ask you to excuse me.' She stood up and looked down at him for a moment before he too rose to his feet and she then found herself looking up at him.

'You're going?' he said, and she couldn't fail to notice the disappointment in his voice.

'I'm afraid so. I have to go home.'

'So where is home? Can I get you a cab…?'

'Home is in Chiswick and I already have a cab booked, thank you.'

'Oh, I see…'

'No doubt we'll see each other around the hospital,' she said.

'Oh, no doubt,' he agreed.

'Goodbye, Mr…er, Nathan.'

'Goodnight, Olivia,' he said softly.

She was only too aware that he stood there in the deep purple shadows of an overhanging wisteria, watching her as she walked across the terrace and into the house.

He stood there for some while after she'd gone, alone but at the same time acutely aware of her presence, which seemed to linger in the soft night air along with the echo of her perfume. She had touched him in some almost inexplicable way, a way that he hadn't experienced in a very long time. There had been something faintly exotic about her, an aura with overtones of some far-flung place, he really wasn't sure where. He only knew that meeting her, talking to her had moved him in some profound way. And now she was gone.

With a sigh he began to move towards the French doors. At least he knew he would see her again, that their paths would cross in the course of their work. His spirits lifted at the prospect then some inner voice urged caution. He knew nothing about her after all, and with the disaster of his failed marriage ever uppermost in his thoughts, he knew he would do well to heed his own self-imposed code of restraint which he had lived by since he and Susan had parted.

As he entered the drawing room, heat, chatter and music assailed his senses, dragging him reluctantly back to reality. Claudia was on the far side of the room and he had just decided he may as well thank her for the evening and take his own leave when he heard Diana's strident tones cut through the atmosphere. 'Claudia,' she called, 'has Olivia gone already?'

'Yes, she has,' Claudia replied, and for some reason Nathan stopped, his senses suddenly alert.

'Oh, so soon?' said Diana. 'I wanted to talk to her again.'

'She needed to get back to the children,' Claudia replied casually. 'Officially it was Helene's day off and she didn't want to take advantage.'

'Oh, well, never mind,' said Diana, but Nathan hardly heard her. Claudia's words had hit him with a dull thud of disappointment. Children. She had children, which probably meant she was married.

Well, what had he expected? he asked himself after he'd taken his leave of Claudia and Rory and settled himself in the back of a cab. A stunning-looking woman like Olivia was bound to be married, or at least accounted for. Not, of course, was that necessarily so—he himself had a son but he was no longer married—but he was clutching at straws now, he knew that. The odds were that she was happily married.

So if that was the case, where was her husband tonight? Why hadn't he come with her? Probably because there was some simple explanation—like he was working, or he was away on business or in the forces or something. No, the best thing he could do was to forget the lovely Olivia and the unexpected impact she'd had on him because if he didn't he felt he would be rushing headlong into all sorts of trouble. And that was the last thing he wanted or needed in his life right now.

It was late when Olivia arrived home, later than she had intended, and after she'd stepped out of the cab and paid the driver she glanced up anxiously at the three-storey, Edwardian

town-house that was her home. Lights were still burning in
the hall and in the top-floor rooms that belonged to Helene.
Quietly she let herself in and from the small, snug room
alongside the large family kitchen at the rear of the house she
heard a familiar series of welcoming thumps. With a little
smile she made her way down the hall, pushed open the
kitchen door and snapped on the light. The thumping sound
ceased, a dark shape appeared in the doorway of the snug and
Oscar, the elderly black Labrador who'd been with Olivia
through thick and thin, stood blinking in the light.

'Hello, old boy.' She crossed the kitchen as the old dog
ambled forward to greet her. 'Did you look after them all for
me?' she said, as she patted his flank and fondled his ears in
just the way he liked. 'Did they behave for you, or did they
lead you a merry dance?' Oscar grunted and nuzzled her hand
then a sound behind her made Olivia turn to find that Helene
had come into the kitchen.

'Helene,' she said, 'I'm sorry. This is later than I had intended—the traffic was heavier than I thought it would be at
this time of night.'

'There is no problem,' Helene lifted her shoulders and
hands, the gesture reinforcing her words. 'I here anyway.'

'Yes, I know, but officially this was your day off—you
must have another evening off to make up for it. Have the
children been all right?'

'They fine. They have supper. They have baths. We have
stories. They go to bed. They asleep now. No problem.'

'Well, thank you, Helene, I really appreciate it.' Olivia
paused. 'Will you have a hot chocolate with me?'

'I get it.' Helene would have turned towards the Aga but
Olivia stopped her.

'No, I'll get it—you sit down.'

Helene sighed but did as she was told while Olivia poured milk into a saucepan and spooned drinking chocolate into two mugs. Whenever she found herself counting her blessings, she always included Helene in the number. The Frenchwoman had originally come to her on an *au pair* scheme seven years ago when Olivia's daughter Charlotte had been born and somehow she had just stayed, long after the time she had been scheduled to return to France, eventually proving herself to be indispensable to the Gilbert family. The crunch had come when Olivia had known she could no longer afford to have a live-in nanny-cum-general help, but her mother-in-law, Grace, had come to the rescue and had paid Helene's wages, enabling Olivia to continue with her career without worrying about the children.

'You have good time?' Helene asked as Olivia waited for the milk to warm.

Olivia lifted her head, reflecting before she answered. She hadn't expected to have a good time, hadn't wanted to go really, but now she felt honour-bound to answer truthfully. 'Actually,' she said, 'yes, I did have a good time. I wasn't expecting to, but I did.'

'That's good.' Helene nodded. 'You need to go out, to mix with people more.'

'Even if they were people from work who I see every day,' Olivia said with a little laugh.

'Even that,' agreed Helene, echoing her laugh. 'Even if you knew them all, it still different away from the hospital.'

There had been one person she hadn't known, she thought as she poured the milk into the mugs. She hadn't met Nathan Carrington until tonight and almost without her realising it she now recognised that he was the reason for her saying she had enjoyed the evening. That last half-hour or so that they had spent together on the terrace had somehow lifted her spirits. But that was as far as it went, as far as it would go, she told herself firmly as she stirred the hot chocolate vigorously and watched it swirl in the mugs. An involvement with anyone, however brief, however fleeting, which had the potential to lead to something more—and deep down she knew with someone like Nathan Carrington that could be the case—was completely and utterly out of the question.

Half an hour later she said goodnight to Helene, made sure Oscar was in his bed in the snug then made her way up the stairs. On the first-floor landing she gently pushed open her son's bedroom door. In the dim glow from the small nightlight beside his bed she could see Lewis, his hair as dark as her own, in stark contrast to the whiteness of his pillow, one arm clutching his toy elephant, the other flung out across the bed. Bending over, she gently kissed his cheek, straightened his duvet then stood for a moment watching him as he slept, the dark lashes resting on his slightly flushed cheeks. As always, her heart suffused with love.

Moments later, when she opened her daughter's bedroom door to repeat the procedure, it was a different story. 'Mummy?' A blonde tousled head was raised from the pillow.

'Charlotte, why aren't you asleep?' whispered Olivia, going right into the room and pushing the door to behind her in order not to disturb Lewis. She knew what Charlotte's answer would be before her daughter replied.

'I wanted to wait until you came in.'

That old anxiety, that somehow she would go out and not come back, just like her father had done. Sitting on the edge of the bed, Olivia drew the little girl into her arms and hugged her. 'I'm home now,' she said softly.

'Was it a nice party?' Charlotte's eyes shone in the half-light.

'Yes, very nice,' said Olivia. 'Auntie Claudia sends her love.'

'What colour was her dress?' demanded Charlotte.

'A sort of dark pink,' said Olivia.

'And did she like your dress?'

'Yes, I think she did.' Olivia paused. 'Did Lewis go to bed all right?'

'We couldn't find Nellie,' said Charlotte.

'Well, he's got her now…'

'Yes, I found her in the end. She was under his bed—and do you know, there was a sweet stuck to her trunk. It was all sticky so Helene washed it.'

'Well, that was good,' said Olivia with a smile. 'Now, darling, you really must get to sleep.'

'All right, Mummy, night-night.' The little girl snuggled down under the covers, happy to go to sleep now that her mother was safely home.

'Night-night, darling. Sleep well.' Olivia kissed her daughter then slipped out of the bedroom, aware that the child was asleep almost instantly.

Losing their father when they had, at such young ages, had been a tremendous trauma in their lives and Olivia knew that the repercussions would echo down the years. Her own devastation had been just as complete, from the very moment when the police had rung the doorbell to tell her of the road traffic accident in which her husband, Marcus, had been killed, through the dreadful dark days that had followed and the funeral, right through until the attempt to rebuild her shattered life and the lives of her children.

But even all that, devastating and traumatic as it had all been, somehow, inexplicably, had not been as much of a shock as what had followed. And the effects of that still had the power to reduce her to a nervous wreck even now, two years later.

With a little sigh Olivia walked along the passage to her own bedroom, leaving the door ajar behind her so that she would hear if either of the children woke up in the night frightened by their dreams.

CHAPTER TWO

'DR GILBERT, Special Care Baby Unit have just called through to ask if you could go down to Theatre. There's a Caesarean section due to take place and John Norris, the obstetrician, has requested the presence of a paediatrician.'

'Thanks, Trudy.' Olivia smiled at the temp who was standing in for her secretary who was on holiday. 'Tell them I'll be right down.'

'Oh, and the other thing.' Trudy consulted her pad. 'There's a case conference at midday on Sara Middleton in Richard Parker's office.'

'I certainly will be there for that,' replied Olivia. 'Sara has been my patient for a long time.' She stood up and moved out from behind her desk. 'Well, if I'm not needed here for the moment, I'll go and get scrubbed up.' Her office was on the floor that housed the paediatric wards, maternity and obstetrics and the special care baby unit, and was very much at the centre of all activity. Her friend, Kirstin Chandler, senior sister in charge of Paediatrics, always firmly maintained that there was very little that happened on the third floor of St Benedict's that Olivia didn't know about.

Now, as Olivia made her way through the children's ward

en route for the unit's theatre, Kirstin popped her head round her own office door.

'Hi,' she said. 'Good weekend?'

'Hello, Kirstin.' Olivia paused. 'Yes, pretty good, thanks. And you?'

'Oh, you know, the usual—the kids wanted a barbeque, Malc wanted to play golf, my mother wanted me to take her shopping… I'm exhausted…'

'Nothing new there, then,' said Olivia with a smile.

'What was the party like?' asked Kirstin curiously. Olivia had told her where she was going on the Saturday night.

'Very good, actually. Yes, I enjoyed it.'

'And there was you not even wanting to go.'

'I know…well, you know me…' Olivia shrugged.

'I'm glad you had a good time. You need to get out more.'

'That's what Helene said,' Olivia replied wryly.

'She's absolutely right,' said Kirstin.

'I don't know.' Olivia shook her head. 'Somehow I'm just not up to it, not really interested in socialising these days.'

'But you enjoyed the party?' persisted Kirstin.

'No one could really fail to enjoy a Lathwell-Foxe party,' said Olivia lightly.

'Rory was in here just now.' Kirstin lowered her voice and glanced over her shoulder. 'He looked shattered.'

'I can't think why.' Olivia laughed. 'They had caterers in.'

'I wish I could have had caterers in for our barbeque,' Kirstin sniffed. 'I just threw it all together and the neighbours came round and all the kids' friends and Malc cooked the sausages and steaks.'

'And I bet you all had a lovely time.'

'Er…yes, we did, actually,' Kirstin agreed.

'Which just goes to prove you don't have to have gallons of champagne, smoked salmon and strawberries and a mansion overlooking the Thames.'

'No, of course not…but I wouldn't say no to all that once in a while…'

Olivia was still smiling as she left Kirstin and continued on her way through the children's ward. This was her world, her work, the work she loved, and as she greeted one child, acknowledged the wave of another and exchanged a brief word with a member of staff, she reflected that along with her own children it was her work that had got her through the last two years. She was passionate about her job, almost as passionate as she had been about her marriage, one had been so cruelly snatched away—thank God she still had the other.

Leaving the ward, she walked a short corridor then entered the hushed, almost hallowed area of Theatre, where she headed for the scrub rooms, changed into theatre greens and secured her hair inside a cap before scrubbing up. By the time she donned her mask and entered Theatre, the theatre team was in place and the patient was being wheeled in.

'Ah, Olivia.' John Norris, the consultant obstetrician, moved away from the patient and the rest of the team in order to speak to her.

'Good morning, John,' she said. 'What do you have for me?'

The obstetrician consulted his notes. 'Patient is Julie Munns, thirty-seven years old, and this is her third baby. Gestation is thirty-five weeks but the baby is struggling so we've decided to proceed with a Caesarean section.'

'Were her other children born by Caesarean?' asked Olivia.

'No.' John shook his head. 'We could have induced for a

natural birth but the baby's heartbeat is irregular and I think it would have been too much.'

'Shall I have a word with her?' asked Olivia.

'Yes, please.' John nodded. 'Her husband is with her.'

Olivia moved across the room to where members of the theatre staff were positioning a screen across Julie so that her husband could sit beside her and hold her hand but at the same time they could both be shielded from what was happening.

'Hello, Julie.' Olivia smiled down at the patient. 'I'm Dr Gilbert. I'm a paediatrician and I will be on hand to examine your baby as soon as it's born.'

'He will be all right, won't he, Doctor?' asked Julie, the anxiety in her eyes plain for everyone to see. 'They said he was struggling and that's why I have to have a Caesarean.'

'That's right,' said Olivia, keeping her voice as matter-of-fact as possible. 'That's far better than the baby, and you, having to work so hard. So tell me.' She looked quickly from Julie to her husband, who was sitting beside her, the expression in his eyes wary with uncertainty. 'You know it's a boy, do you?'

'Yes.' Julie nodded. 'I had a scan earlier on. We didn't think we wanted to know but when they asked us, suddenly we couldn't resist it, could we, Dave?' She turned her head and looked at her husband.

'No,' he agreed, 'we couldn't. We have two girls and we really want a boy...' He trailed off, seemingly unable to continue.

'You will do all you can for our baby, won't you, Doctor?' whispered Julie.

'Of course we will.' Olivia gave her a reassuring smile. 'Please, try not to worry. We have a wonderful team here at St Benedict's and I can assure you that everything possible will be done. Now, Julie, you've had your epidural so just try and relax.'

Olivia stepped back into the background to allow the obstetrician to make his incision and the theatre team to carry out their duties. When the baby was finally lifted out of his mother's womb the umbilical cord was cut and he was handed to the theatre sister. She carried him to a side table and immediately began to clear his airways, leaving John to deal with the placenta and with the mother.

Moments later Olivia moved forward to carry out her examination of the newborn baby. He looked very small and hadn't made a sound, but as the sister continued to work to clear mucus from his airways there came a series of frantic questions from the baby's parents.

'Is he all right?'

'Why hasn't he cried?'

'Is he breathing?'

As Olivia applied the warmed head of her stethoscope to the baby's tiny chest he suddenly gave a gasp and a thin cry left his bluish lips.

'Oh, he's crying,' choked Julie.

'That means he must be all right,' said Dave.

But as Olivia listened to the baby's heartbeat she frowned and her eyes met those of the theatre sister over the tops of their masks. After Olivia had completed a thorough examination of the baby, checking for abnormalities and possible defects, she carefully lifted the baby from the table and wrapped him in a clean white blanket. 'We need to put him straight into an incubator,' she said, 'and get him down to Special Care.'

'The incubator's ready.' Sister indicated the mobile cot. 'But what about a moment with Mum? Is that possible first?'

'Just for one moment,' Olivia replied, and carried the baby

over to Julie and Dave, very gently placing the child in his mother's arms.

'Only for a minute,' she said warningly, 'then he must go along to Special Care—he needs help with his breathing.'

'Oh, hello, little one,' said Julie, as she received her son into her arms and her husband moved forward in order to see the baby.

'He's a lovely boy,' said Olivia with a smile. 'Do you have a name for him yet?'

'Yes.' It was Dave who answered. 'He's going to be William George—after my dad,' he added proudly, then anxiously he looked up at Olivia and said, 'He is going to be all right, isn't he?'

'We are going to keep a very close eye on him for a while,' Olivia replied gently, 'and we will need to do a few tests.'

'What tests?' asked Dave in alarm. 'What sort of tests?'

'Because he's premature,' said Julie. 'That's right, isn't it, Doctor?'

'Yes, Julie, that's exactly right,' agreed Olivia. Holding out her arms towards the baby she said, 'I'm sorry but we will have to take him now and put him in an incubator.'

'Oh, so soon?' An anguished expression crossed Julie's features.

'I'm afraid so,' said Olivia sympathetically, 'but once Mr Norris has finished with you and you've had a bit of a rest, I'm sure Sister will arrange for you to visit William in Special Care.' Gently Olivia took baby William from his mother and placed him in the incubator then moments later, after a word with John and together with a staff nurse and the theatre porter, she escorted the incubator with its precious passenger out of Theatre and down the corridors to the special care baby unit.

* * *

'Nathan, I'd like you to stand in for me at this case conference.' Richard Parker looked up from behind his desk as Nathan, still in his scrubs from Theatre where he had just carried out a full morning's list, came into the consulting room. 'I have an emergency triple bypass, but from what I can see from the notes, this conference really shouldn't be delayed. Sorry to land you in it, but it's just one of those things, I'm afraid.'

'That's all right, Richard—all in a day's work,' Nathan replied amiably.

'Even so...' Richard shrugged. 'You won't forget your first week here in a hurry, will you?'

'It's no different to my last job—if anything, that was even more frantic because we were understaffed most of the time. At least here at St Benedict's we have a full team. So tell me, what details do we have about this case conference?'

'It's a child, Sara Middleton. She's been a patient here for some time—born with a hole in the heart. She's becoming increasingly short of breath and it's time to operate, in my opinion, but unfortunately she has other problems—Down's syndrome, asthma and a digestive tract condition. Anyway, the final decision will be down to Victor Quale and the child's paediatrician who, I believe, is Olivia Gilbert. Have you met Olivia yet?'

At mention of her name, an image flashed through Nathan's mind, an image of her moving gracefully through the gardens, one hand extended, gently touching the flowerheads. 'Yes,' he said, forcing himself to concentrate, 'I have, actually. We met at the weekend at Rory's place.'

'Ah, yes,' said Richard. 'I expect that was a good do—sorry I had to miss it.'

'It was good,' Nathan agreed.

'So what did you think of her—the lovely Olivia?' asked Richard.

'Er…just that—lovely,' said Nathan.

'Yes, she is.' Richard nodded. 'She also happens to be a damn good paediatrician.'

Nathan wanted to ask him more about Olivia but somehow he couldn't quite bring himself to do so. He didn't want it to sound as if he was too eager.

After he'd showered and changed out of his scrubs, he made his way back to Richard's room where it had been agreed the case conference would take place. As he crossed the threshold he knew she was already there—sensed her presence before he actually saw her. She was seated in a chair by the window, dressed in a dark suit and a crisp white shirt, her hair drawn back from her face and fastened at the nape of her neck. She was talking to a young male doctor who was seated beside her, but she looked up as Nathan came into the room and for a moment, as their eyes met, she held his gaze. Almost imperceptibly, so that no one else in the room was even aware of it, he inclined his head and she responded like-wise. Then the moment was gone and in a brisk, businesslike way he moved forward and took up his position behind Richard's desk.

'Good afternoon.' He glanced around at the assembled group. 'In case you are wondering, Richard Parker has asked me to stand in and conduct this case conference for him be-cause he is in Theatre. For those of you whom I haven't yet met, my name is Nathan Carrington and I'm on Richard's team. The patient we are discussing is Sara Middleton.' He looked down at the folder on Richard's desk then around at the others. 'Do we have all the relevant notes on this patient?'

He paused and once again his gaze met Olivia's. 'Dr Gilbert, I believe the young lady in question is in your care?'

'Yes, she is.' Olivia nodded and, opening a file, she began taking out notes. 'As I'm sure you are all aware, Sara has Down's syndrome.' She paused. 'She was born with atrio-ventricular defects—a large hole in the muscle partition that divides the chambers of her heart. These are all her recent test results.' She passed the sheaf of papers to Nathan then glanced across the room to the consultant cardiologist, who was seated on the far side, 'Victor, I believe you also have relevant re-sults…'

'Yes.' Victor Quale glanced down at his own notes. 'We do, and in my opinion this patient is now ready for surgery—in fact, I would go so far as to say that her need has become crucial and surgery is now a priority.'

'Are you in agreement with that, Dr Gilbert?' asked Nathan, raising his eyebrows slightly in Olivia's direction.

'Yes, I am,' she agreed. 'I had been hoping that we could have waited longer but, as Mr Quale has just said, the case has now become urgent so I feel the only answer is to proceed as soon as possible.'

'Do we have any social reports on Sara?' asked Nathan.

'Yes.' Saskia Nkombo, Sara's Social Worker, spoke up. 'Sara's situation is as good as it will ever be—mother is a single parent who has two other children younger than Sara. The family live on state benefits and they receive help from carers and the respite centre. The whole family are very supportive of Sara. But lately, of course, Sara has been spending more and more time in the children's ward as her condition has worsened.'

After further discussion and some time studying the girl's

notes, Nathan looked up. 'From what you are all saying and, given the results of the tests, it is my opinion that Sara should be put on a high-priority surgical list and a date arranged for her operation. Is everyone of the same opinion?' There were nods and murmurs of assent as once again he looked round at the others.

'Good.' He nodded. 'Does anyone else have anything they wish to discuss?'

'Just one thing.' Victor spoke up. 'Dr Gilbert and I have just examined a baby on the special care unit—eight weeks premature, Caesarean section, will require surgery in the next few days to close a hole in his heart. We had intended asking Mr Parker if he would have a look at him, but as Mr Parker is unavailable at the moment, maybe you would go down, Mr Carrington?'

'Yes, of course.' Nathan nodded. 'I'd also like to see Sara as there's a possibility I'll be the one operating on her. Maybe, Dr Gilbert, you would take me to see both children?'

'Certainly,' Olivia replied.

'Well, if there's no other business,' Nathan concluded, 'we'll bring this meeting to a close.'

As the rest of the staff filed from the room, Nathan was aware that Olivia lingered. 'Would you like to see the children now?' she said.

'Do you have the time?'

She glanced at her watch, 'Yes,' she said, 'I think so—just about.'

'In that case…' Leaving the sentence unfinished, he fell into step beside her.

'How are you settling in?' she asked, throwing him a sideways glance as they began to walk the long corridors that connected the cardiac unit with Paediatrics.

'Pretty well—I think. Richard fazed me a bit asking me to take the case conference—it's difficult to sound intelligent and articulate when not only do you not know the patients involved but you also haven't met half the staff as well.'

'You did very well,' Olivia said, 'and you'd already met me.'

'Yes,' he agreed. 'I'd met you, and I have to say that was quite a relief. It did my confidence good to see a familiar face in that room, I can tell you.' He paused. 'I have to confess I'm really not into meetings and the administration side of things—I really come into my own in Theatre.'

'I can understand that,' Olivia replied. 'Unfortunately the administration side seems to be playing a bigger part in our work these days.'

They walked in silence for a while then Nathan spoke again. 'You obviously got home safely after Claudia's party?' he said.

'Oh, yes,' she replied. 'I always use the same cab firm—I know them and they know me.'

'That makes a difference.' He wanted to ask about her children but he didn't want her to think that others had been talking about her after she'd left the party, and while he was still trying to phrase the question they reached the paediatric unit.

'We'll just have a word with Sister,' said Olivia. Pausing at Kirstin's office, she tapped on the door then opened it. 'Hello, Kirstin,' she said. 'I've brought Mr Carrington to meet Sara—is that convenient?'

Nathan was aware of a short, curvy woman with a mass of dark curls and a happy expression then Olivia was making the necessary introductions. 'Nathan, this is Sister Kirstin Chandler—the children's ward is her domain. Kirstin, this is

Nathan Carrington—he's the new consultant on Richard Parker's firm.'

They shook hands and exchanged pleasantries then Kirstin's eyes narrowed slightly as her gaze shifted from Nathan to Olivia. 'So, has a decision been reached on Sara?' she asked.

Nathan glanced at Olivia and nodded, and it was she who gave Kirstin her answer. 'Yes,' she said. 'It was agreed at the case conference that we proceed with surgery at the earliest opportunity. Nathan is possibly the one who'll be carrying out the surgery—that's why he wants to see Sara.'

'I'm delighted a decision has been agreed,' said Kirstin, then, looking at Nathan, she said, 'Come with me. I'll take you to meet Sara.'

'How is she today?' asked Olivia.

'She's having one of her better days,' Kirstin replied guardedly as she led the way out of her office. The walls of the ward were covered in brightly coloured murals of scenes from Disney films, while the repetitive sounds of a well-known pop song, which had dominated the music charts for weeks, filled the air, along with the chatter and laughter of the children and the staff.

'Does she know she is to have surgery?' asked Nathan.

'We've talked about it,' said Olivia, 'but I don't think she has any concept of what surgery actually means.'

'So remind me,' murmured Nathan as they began to make their way through the ward. 'She has Down's syndrome, and she's, what, eleven years old?'

'No, twelve,' Kirstin replied. 'She's had a lot to contend with in those twelve years, as you will have realised from her notes, but she's the happiest, sunniest child you could ever wish to meet.'

'Is anyone with her today?' asked Olivia.

'Yes, her mother, Sharon, is with her,' said Kirstin, as they reached an area at the end of the ward where several children were busy playing with poster paints and large sheets of paper in the charge of a young care worker. 'Hello, Jackie.' Kirstin smiled at the carer. 'We have some visitors for Sara.'

Sara had her back to them but at Kirstin's words she turned and Nathan recognised the characteristic signs of her condition. 'Hello, Kirstin,' she said, and a beaming smile lit up her face. 'I'm painting a picture.'

'Oh, Sara, that's lovely,' said Kirstin, then turned to a woman who sat a little apart from the children and said, 'Sharon, this is Mr Carrington. He's come to see Sara.'

'What for?' There was a touch of alarm in the woman's eyes.

'Let me have a word with Sharon,' said Olivia, moving forward so that she could sit beside the girl's mother and explain the situation, leaving Nathan free to talk to Sara.

'Sara, are you going to show Mr Carrington your painting?' said Kirstin.

'Yes, all right,' said Sara in her rather gruff little voice, 'but I wanted to show it to Olivia really.'

'Well, you can in a minute, but Olivia is talking to Mummy first.'

'Oh, I see,' said Sara. Peering up at Nathan through her glasses, she said, 'I'm painting a princess.'

'That's wonderful, Sara. May I see?' Nathan crouched down beside her and studied the coloured blobs and lines on the sheet of paper in front of Sara. 'Is that the princess?' he said, pointing to a particularly large pink shape.

Sara hooted with mirth. 'No,' she cried, clapping both hands over her mouth, 'that's a dragon.'

'Oh,' said Nathan. 'A dragon. Of course it is. Silly me. I can see it's a dragon now. So has the dragon captured the princess?'

Another hoot of laughter came from Sara and this time the other children around the table, all much younger than Sara, joined in. 'No,' she said, 'it's her pet dragon!'

'Of course it is.' Nathan peered more closely then realised that Sara was no longer looking at her picture but was peering intently at him.

'What's your name?' she said.

'Nathan,' he replied.

'That's a funny name.'

'Yes,' he agreed, 'it is rather, isn't it?'

'My name's Sara,' she said.

'Yes,' he said, turning his head so that his face was only inches away from hers. 'That's a lovely name.'

'I know,' she said. 'Olivia's a lovely name, too.'

'Yes,' he agreed, 'it is.'

'I like Olivia. She's my friend. Do you like Olivia?'

'Yes,' he said, 'I like Olivia.'

'Is she your friend?' asked Sara, and the beaming smile was replaced by an anxious frown.

'I hope she is,' he replied solemnly, hoping that Sara would leave it there, but obviously she had other ideas. Twisting round in her chair, she looked towards her mother and Olivia, who were still talking together.

'Olivia,' she called.

'Yes, Sara, what is it?' Olivia looked up quickly and for the briefest of moments Nathan felt the breath catch in his throat. What was it about this woman that seemed to have such an effect on him?

'Are you Nathan's friend?' asked Sara, and Nathan again caught the trace of anxiety in her voice.

'Yes, of course I am.' Olivia's reply was without hesitation.

'That's good.' Sara nodded with apparent satisfaction then, turning back to Nathan, she said, 'It's all right. Olivia says she is your friend.'

'I'm very pleased about that,' said Nathan, and briefly his gaze met Olivia's, holding it until she coloured slightly and looked away.

'I like Olivia,' said Sara again. 'She's ever so nice.'

'Sara.' Nathan took a deep breath. 'I'm going to go and talk to your mum now. Shall I ask Olivia to come and see you?'

'Yes, all right,' Sara said in a matter-of-fact fashion.

Nathan rose to his feet and walked across to Olivia and Sharon. 'Hello, Mrs Middleton,' he said. 'I'm Nathan Carrington.'

'Sara's let you go, then,' said Olivia with a faint smile.

'Only on the condition that you go and talk to her while I talk to her mother,' he replied with a rueful grin.

'In that case, I'd better do so.'

As Olivia moved away towards the children's table Nathan turned to Sharon, but before he could speak she said, 'Will it be you who does Sara's operation?'

'Most probably.' He nodded. 'We are going to fit her in as soon as possible, but I'm sure Dr Gilbert will have explained all that to you.'

'Yes, she has,' Sharon replied. 'Dr Gilbert has been wonderful with Sara all along.'

'I'm sure she has.' Nathan nodded again. 'I was wondering,' he went on after a moment, 'if you have any questions you want to ask me?'

'Just one.' Sharon's eyes misted over. 'This operation really is necessary, isn't it?'

'Yes, Mrs Middleton,' he replied, his voice gentle, 'it really is.'

'I know there's a risk.' She gulped. 'That there's a risk with any operation. But I would hate to think that we took that risk if it wasn't really necessary.'

'It is necessary,' he said softly, 'and I can assure you we will do everything in our power to minimise the risk to Sara.'

'She's very precious to me…'

'Of course she is. I do understand,' he added.

'Do you?' She looked up. 'Do you really? Do you have children?'

'Yes,' he said. 'I have a son, Jamie, and I know I would be feeling exactly the same as you if our positions were reversed. Now the decision has been made, we will keep you fully informed of what is happening and we'll let you know just as soon as we have a date.'

'Thank you, Mr Carrington.' Sharon wiped away a stray tear and Nathan made his way back to Olivia.

'I think,' he said, 'we need to move on to Special Care, if that's all right with you.'

'Yes, of course.' Olivia straightened up and rescued her stethoscope from Sara, who had whipped it out of the pocket of her suit and was applying it to the chest of a large teddy bear who was seated amongst the other children. 'Thanks, Sara,' Olivia said. 'We have to go now.'

'Will you come and see me again?' asked Sara.

'Yes, of course,' Olivia replied.

'And Dr Nathan?'

'Yes, and Dr Nathan.'

'That's good,' said Sara. 'Dr Nathan's my friend...'

They made their exit and were still smiling when they reached the corridor. 'She's a delightful child,' said Nathan, as they headed in the direction of Special Care.

'Yes, she is,' Olivia agreed. 'But she does get anxious if something as she perceives it is not quite right.'

'Like if someone she thought to be her friend turns out not to be?' He raised his eyebrows.

'Exactly.' Olivia nodded. 'We always do all we can to minimise her anxieties.' She paused then glancing up at Nathan, she said, 'You were obviously a hit with her.'

'I hope so.' He laughed then, growing serious again, he said, 'Her mother was understandably very anxious about the forthcoming surgery. I hope I was able to allay her fears.'

'It's been a long and difficult haul with Sara,' Olivia admitted, 'and it's been especially difficult for Sharon, having to deal with it on her own.'

'What happened to her husband?'

'Hard to say really.' Olivia shrugged. 'But from what Sharon has told me, I would say it looks like he was never able to fully come to terms with Sara's condition.'

'But there are other children, aren't there?' said Nathan quickly.

'Yes, two others who are both all right. I think they thought that other children would help to restore the balance and possibly save the marriage, which was already rocky.'

'But it didn't?'

'No, unfortunately.' Olivia shook her head. 'Things deteriorated rapidly after the birth of the third child and the husband left shortly afterwards.'

'Leaving Sharon to cope on her own?'

'Sadly, yes. We see this so often in paediatrics, how caring for a disabled child puts a strain on the whole family—and especially on the parents' relationship.'

'Does Sharon receive adequate support?'

'Her own family is supportive—her mother and sisters and, surprisingly, her mother-in-law, who is devoted to Sara.'

'Well, I suppose that's something, but it's still very rough on Sharon.'

'Yes, quite,' Olivia said, then slowed down and indicated the entrance to the special care baby unit. 'Here we are,' she said. 'This is like stepping into another world. We'll need to scrub and put on gowns and masks.'

Nathan followed her as they gained entry to the unit and as they were greeted by the sister in charge it struck him how totally dedicated Olivia seemed to her job and to the children in her care.

CHAPTER THREE

IT WAS quite true what she'd said—stepping into Special Care really was like entering another world, a world apart from the rest of the hospital, a world of high-tech equipment and ultra-sterile conditions, with its team of highly trained staff whose sole purpose was the care and welfare of—for the most part—the tiny premature babies entrusted to them.

'Hello, Rosemary.' Olivia stopped at the scrubbing-up area. 'I've brought Mr Carrington to see baby William.' She half turned to Nathan, who was standing behind her. 'Nathan, this is Sister Rosemary Morris. Rosemary, Nathan Carrington, who has just joined Richard Parker's team.'

After exchanging greetings, Rosemary said, 'After you've scrubbed up, I'll take you along to see baby William.'

'How is he?' asked Olivia.

'Struggling,' Rosemary answered, 'but he's a little fighter and he's still holding his own.'

'Are his parents with him?' asked Olivia as she began applying the antiseptic solution to her hands used to cleanse the skin then passed the bottle to Nathan.

'His father is,' Rosemary replied, 'but Mum is up on Postnatal recovering. I expect they'll bring her down to see him later.'

Moments later, after donning gowns and masks, Olivia and Nathan followed Rosemary to the high-dependency wing on Special Care. There were four incubator cots in the room, together with a mass of high-technology equipment. Dave Munns, also dressed in gown and mask, was sitting alongside one of the cots, gazing at the tiny baby inside. As they approached, Olivia could see that the baby, naked except for a nappy and a minute woolly hat, was wired up to a heart monitor, and as they stopped at the foot of the incubator Dave looked up. 'Oh, Dr Gilbert,' he said, and would have stood up but Olivia held out her hand.

'Don't get up, Dave,' she said, then as Dave's gaze moved to Nathan, she went on, 'Has Mr Quale been to see you yet?'

Dave nodded and Olivia noticed that his eyes were red-rimmed, as if he'd been crying. 'He's the heart man, isn't he?' asked Dave, and when Olivia nodded he said, 'Yes, he spoke to Julie and myself up on the postnatal ward after he'd examined William.'

'What did he tell you?' asked Olivia gently, looking down at the baby as she spoke. Almost as if he knew he was the centre of discussion, the baby opened his eyes, yawned and stretched then closed his eyes again and retreated back into his own little world.

'He said William would need an operation—he has a hole in his heart and it has to be closed...' Once again he glanced up at Nathan.

'That's right,' Olivia said. She hadn't wanted to alarm Dave by introducing the surgeon if he was still unaware that his son needed corrective surgery. 'This is Mr Carrington,' she explained. 'He's a cardiac surgeon and he'll most probably be carrying out the operation on William.'

'Oh, right.' Dave blinked as if events were moving too swiftly for him to take in.

'Hello, there.' Nathan moved forward so that he could see the baby. 'So this is the young man in question,' he added.

'Yes,' said Dave, 'this is William.' He paused—a silence laden with unspoken anxiety—then hesitantly, but with utter simplicity, said, 'He will be all right, won't he?'

'We will do everything in our power to make sure he is,' replied Nathan quietly.

'And he really does need this operation?' Dave's anxiety echoed that of Sharon's as he also sought confirmation of the necessity for his child's surgery.

'Yes, Mr Munns.' Nathan stepped in swiftly so there would be no ambiguity over the decision that had already been taken. 'William really does need surgery to close the hole in his heart.'

'And if he doesn't have it?' Dave appeared to brace himself as if he already knew the answer.

'We would not be able to save him.' Nathan's reply was blunt and direct but at the same time steeped in compassion, and as Dave's eyes closed in resignation he added, 'Provided we operate soon, there is every reason to believe that William will make a full recovery.'

'But there's still a risk. Dr Quale said there was a degree of risk with every operation...'

'And he's quite right,' Nathan agreed, 'but the risk of not operating is far, far greater.'

'When would you...when would you do it?' Almost as if he couldn't bring himself to utter the word 'operate', Dave looked down at the tiny form in the cot.

Nathan glanced at Olivia who nodded. 'Within the next few days,' he replied.

'As soon as that!' Dave's head jerked up and he looked astounded.

'We shouldn't delay for too long.'

'But he's so tiny,' Dave protested. His shoulders slumped, but after a moment's silence he seemed to draw himself up. 'Well,' he said at last, 'if it has to be done, then it has to be done.' He hesitated. 'Have you told Julie yet?'

'No, not yet.' Olivia shook her head. 'Would you like us to tell her or would you?'

'I think I'll tell her,' said Dave, then, glancing up at Nathan, he added, 'But she may well want to speak to you afterwards.'

'Of course,' said Nathan. 'I'll arrange to see you together then I can explain the surgical procedure and what you can expect.'

'Thank you.' Dave hauled himself to his feet and faced Nathan, 'Thank you, Mr…er…'

'Mr Carrington,' said Olivia as Dave floundered to remember the right name.

'Yes. Mr Carrington. Thank you, thank you very much.'

With a final, reassuring smile at Dave, Olivia led the way out of the high-dependency wing. 'There's a man who's had the bottom drop out of his world,' she observed to Nathan.

'Yes,' he agreed. 'It must be such an emotional roller-coaster, all the build-up to the birth then this numbing anxiety afterwards.'

He sounded as if he knew, as if he really identified or at least really cared, but somehow Olivia doubted that he could truly empathise with Dave's situation. Maybe that was unfair because she knew nothing about Nathan, but somehow he hadn't come across as a family man—more as someone who worked hard, played hard and enjoyed the finer things in life,

which, of course, his salary was able to provide. By this time
they were back in the main area of the special care unit, where
they disrobed, washed their hands and took their leave of
Rosemary and her team.

'I need to get back to Paediatrics,' said Olivia as they
walked back down the corridors.

'And I to Theatre,' he replied, glancing at his watch.

'Thank you for taking the time and trouble with Sara and
William,' she said as they reached the entrance to the children's
ward.

'Not at all. It's all part of the service.'

'I wish all surgeons felt that way,' she replied lightly.
Briefly, just briefly, she allowed her gaze to meet his.

He shrugged lightly. 'Keep me posted on both of them.'

'Yes, of course.' Then he was gone. Just for one moment
she watched him as he strode away down the corridor then
thoughtfully she turned and entered the children's ward. He
really was rather nice, she thought. If she had been looking
to start a relationship, he might, just might have been the type
she would have looked for. But, then, what did she know
about types? What did anyone know about someone on short
acquaintance or even, come to that, on lengthy acquaintance?
Was anyone ever really sure about anyone else? She had no
answers. Once upon a time she might have thought she had,
but now she really didn't know, doubted, in fact, whether she
could trust her own judgement ever again.

'Hey.' Kirstin pounced the moment Olivia entered the
ward. 'Where on earth have you been hiding him?'

'Who?' Olivia frowned but she had a vague idea to whom
her friend was referring.

'Who, she says.' Kirstin threw up her hands. 'Only the

dishiest hunk to have crossed our threshold in the last hundred years—why, the man positively smoulders!'

'I gather you mean Nathan Carrington?' said Olivia coolly.

'Is there another?' said Kirstin with a little sigh.

'Well, I can assure you I haven't been hiding him,' said Olivia briskly. 'Let's face it, there aren't too many occasions, thank heavens, when we need the services of a cardiac surgeon on this ward.'

'That's true,' Kirstin agreed, 'but I have to say, you seemed to be getting on rather well with him—for someone you'd just met, that is.'

'Actually...' said Olivia, then trailed off.

'Yes?' Kirstin seized on her slight hesitation. 'Actually, what?'

'We'd already met.'

'Oh, yes?' Kirstin raised a speculative eyebrow. 'And when was this?'

'He was at Rory and Claudia's party—we had a bit of a chat.'

'Hmm, you never said.'

'I didn't think I had to.' Olivia laughed. 'Honestly, Kirstin, it was no big deal, I can assure you. You know me where men are concerned—I'm simply not interested.'

'Probably just as well—at least where that particular man is concerned.'

'Oh, and why is that?' In spite of herself, she was curious as to what Kirstin meant.

'Well, for a start, he's married.'

'Is he?' Olivia felt a pang somewhere deep inside that felt suspiciously like the closing of a door.

'You didn't know?' asked Kirstin, and when Olivia shook

her head she said, 'Jackie heard him tell Sharon Middleton that he has a son.'

'I didn't know that either,' said Olivia slowly, 'but I guess it figures—like you say, he is a bit of a hunk and it stands to reason that he would be accounted for.'

'Pity really.' Kirstin eyed her thoughtfully as she spoke.

'Kirstin…' she began warningly.

'Oh, I know what you said, Olivia,' said Kirstin with a sniff, 'but I think it's a crying shame. You're young and lovely and I'm certain Marcus wouldn't have wanted you to spend the rest of your life on your own.'

At the mention of Marcus Olivia felt something tighten inside her—just like it always did.

'You need to get out more, speaking of which you'll be coming to the fun day the hospital social club is putting on for the children for Father's Day, won't you?'

'Oh, I don't know, Kirstin.' Olivia shook her head. 'That's not exactly something we observe in our household any more.' A mental picture of Charlotte weeping hysterically the previous year because she could no longer buy a card and a present for Marcus suddenly entered her head.

'I know,' said Kirstin sympathetically. 'But I still think you should come.'

'I don't think it would be right for Charlotte and Lewis—I think it would be best to simply ignore it.'

'You can't pretend it isn't happening,' said Kirstin gently. 'It's advertised everywhere, on the telly, in the shops, and it's something you'll have to contend with every year. Honestly, Olivia, I think the sooner the children get to grips with that, the better it will be for them. And it will be good fun—

they'll enjoy it. The committee have organised all sorts of things.'

'Well, maybe, we'll see,' said Olivia, but she still sounded doubtful. Then, in a determined attempt to change the subject, she said, 'Now, Kirstin, don't you have a child for me to see who was admitted this morning with an asthma attack?'

'Yes, I do.' Kirstin gave a little sigh and led the way through the ward.

So he's married, Olivia thought as later that day she drove home from St Benedict's to Chiswick. She'd been wrong in her assumption that he was single. Not, of course, that that should make any difference whatsoever to her professional relationship with him. She had, however, been reasonably certain that the interest he'd shown in her hadn't been altogether professional, something which now made her all the more determined to keep him at arm's length. Involvement of any description was the last thing she wanted, let alone any involvement with a married man.

With that thought uppermost in her mind, she parked her car and let herself into the house. From upstairs came the sound of Charlotte practising her recorder and from outside in the garden at the rear of the house she could hear Lewis as he shouted and threw sticks for Oscar to retrieve.

Helene was in the kitchen and she looked up with her ready smile as Olivia set down her case and sank down into a chair. 'Busy day?' she said sympathetically.

'You could say that.' Olivia nodded. 'How about you? Everything all right?'

It was the question she always asked, a question which in the early days she had dreaded the answer to, imagining that all sorts of disasters must have befallen her children in her absence. But as time had gone on, her confidence in Helene's ability to look after them had grown.

'Everything fine,' said Helene. Crossing to the fridge, she took out a carton and poured orange juice into a glass, which she set before Olivia on the kitchen table.

'Thanks, Helene,' said Olivia gratefully, and took a mouthful.

'I take Charlotte to the dentist after school—everything fine,' she said quickly, before Olivia could ask. 'Lewis bring home letter about parent evenings—I put it on the board.' She pointed to the large corkboard on the wall, which was a vital form of communication in the household.

'Thank you, Helene,' said Olivia. 'Now, I guess I'd better catch up with the children.' She stood up, drained her glass and was just placing it in the dishwasher when Charlotte suddenly appeared in the kitchen doorway.

'I didn't know you were home!' she exclaimed, then hurled herself at her mother.

'I've only just come in,' said Olivia, kissing the top of Charlotte's head. 'Helene was telling me about your dental appointment.'

'He was very pleased with me,' said Charlotte proudly. 'And I've got a new toothbrush—it's pink and it has diamonds on the handle. Helene said they were real diamonds, didn't you, Helene?'

'What else they be?' Helene shrugged her shoulders and smiled.

'I want you to hear me play my recorder,' said Charlotte excitedly. 'I can play "Twinkle, Twinkle, Little Star", can't I, Helene?'

'Yes, she can,' Helene agreed.

'I want you to come and hear me now.' Charlotte began tugging at Olivia's sleeve.

'Let your mother catch her breath,' said Helene.

'Well, will you after that?' Charlotte pouted.

'I will when I've been to say hello to Lewis,' said Olivia firmly.

'I'll go and get him,' said Charlotte, and scampered out of the room.

Helene rolled her eyes and went back to preparing the children's tea. Seconds later Lewis burst noisily into the room and launched himself into Olivia's arms.

'Hello, darling.' Briefly she buried her face in his mass of black curls. 'Had a good day?'

'OK.' He shrugged. 'You mustn't say darling any more,' he said suddenly, as if something had just occurred to him.

'Oh?' said Olivia. 'And why is that?'

'Alfie says it's sissy.'

'And who is Alfie?'

'He's a new boy in my class.'

'I see. Do you like him?'

'Not much,' admitted Lewis with a frown, 'but he'll say I'm a sissy if you call me darling.'

'Tell you what,' said Olivia, 'I promise I will only call you darling at home, when none of your friends are around. Is that OK?'

'I suppose so,' said Lewis doubtfully.

The following hour or so was taken up with listening to Charlotte's recorder practice, supervising her homework, listening to Lewis read then sitting with them while they ate their tea and shared the day's news. It wasn't until both children were bathed and in bed and she'd read stories to them then poured herself a glass of wine that Olivia remembered the fun day that Kirstin had mentioned, and she sat for some time staring out of the window, wondering what she should do. The last thing she wanted was that a celebration for Father's Day should only reinforce the sad fact to her own children that they no longer had a father. On the other hand, as Kirstin had so rightly pointed out, they could hardly fail to notice the fact that those children who did have fathers celebrated the day and would continue to do so every year. Maybe it would be better to confront this now and deal with it rather than pretend it wasn't happening and store up trouble for later. And there was no denying the fact that the children would probably have a good time.

Idly she found herself wondering about Nathan and whether or not his wife and family would also be there. At one time, when Marcus had been alive, there would have been no question, no hesitation over whether or not they would go to such an event—it would quite simply have been taken as read that they would have done so. But that had been then, over two years ago when the children had been small—Charlotte only five and Lewis at three little more than a toddler. That had been when they had been a family, happy and secure, before death had crossed their path…and… She stood up and gripped the window-sill, her knuckles showing white. And before that other thing had happened…that dreadful thing, which she had been unable to bring herself to speak of to anyone, even now, after all this time.

Maybe she should have told someone, maybe she still should. But who would understand? Who would appreciate the pain and anguish that she'd gone through, pain and anguish that had been separate from her grief? She could hardly tell anyone in the family, couldn't really burden any of them with it. After all, they had their own grief to contend with, especially Marcus's mother Grace, and her own parents, all of whom had been pretty devastated at his sudden and tragic death. She'd once considered telling Claudia but when it had come to the moment had found herself opting out, unable to put it into words. Likewise, just briefly she'd been on the brink of telling Kirstin, then had thought better of it.

Maybe one day she would tell someone. Maybe one day there would be a right moment and a right person to confide in, but until that moment came she would remain silent.

As Nathan prepared his solitary supper that night, he reflected that he still couldn't quite believe that Jamie was actually going to come to London and spend the whole weekend with him. He saw so little of the boy these days that when an opportunity like this arose, it seemed like a stroke of luck. It had all been so different once, but that seemed like another lifetime now—those days before he and Susan had parted. He'd adored her once, practically worshipping the very ground she'd walked on, and he'd thought—no, he was sure—she'd felt the same way about him.

They'd met one summer when he'd been on vacation from medical school and had returned to his parents' home to find they had new neighbours. Susan and her parents had come around for drinks and there had been instant attraction between the two of them. He could still see her now and the way she had looked that evening, with her dark hair framing her face and the vibrant red dress she had worn, which had shown off her colouring and figure to such perfection. His father had been as captivated as he had been, but he had sensed a wariness from his mother where Susan was concerned, a wariness which had never left her and which, he thought, she felt had been justified when they'd later parted. But, to give his mother her due, she had never once mentioned it, not then, or when they'd married, or later, when they'd parted.

They had married in a ceremony at the local church, followed by a lavish reception at the best hotel in town, no expense being spared by Susan's parents for their only child. It had been a rather stormy relationship and only now, in retrospect, could he see that was partly because Susan had been so spoilt and indulged as a child that she had seen it as her right for her life to go on in the same way.

For his own part, he also recognised that he had allowed himself to become totally immersed in his studies and his career, forcing Susan into a back-seat position she was neither used to nor able to accept. She complained bitterly about how little time they spent together, a situation he thought might change after Jamie was born, but when Jamie was little more than a year old Susan returned to her job as a PR consultant to an advertising agency, leaving Jamie in the care of her mother. Instead of them growing closer, their paths seemed to diverge even more, and then, when Jamie was four years old, Susan dropped her bombshell and told him that she was leaving him for another man. It was a tremendous blow to Nathan, who later blamed himself for not having seen it coming. At first he was angry, but as time went on and his anger subsided, it was his father who eventually persuaded him to let go and try to pick up the pieces of his life.

Custody of Jamie went to Susan and much as it hurt Nathan to let his son go, he reluctantly agreed that it was for the best as he knew that with his career and the often irregular hours he was forced to work, he wouldn't be able to provide the continuity of care that the boy needed.

In some ways he'd been able to take his father's advice and get on with his life. The anger passed but the sense of betrayal remained with him and the pain and bitterness of that was a constant reminder, but just lately he'd found himself thinking that it really was time to move on.

He'd been out with a few women since his divorce, of course he had, but deep in his heart he knew the one thing that was missing in all these brief relationships was his ability to trust again. He was attracted to Olivia, he knew that just as he knew that if he'd been able to ask her out, get to know her further, he might still have been faced with the problem of not being able to trust her. Maybe it was just as well that he'd found out she was married, unavailable, so now he would never have to put himself to that test where she was concerned.

Home for Nathan since moving to London was an apartment near the docks in a converted warehouse. It was small and cost an absolute fortune but suited his needs and was a reasonable distance from the hospital. Jamie hadn't yet seen it and he found himself looking forward to the experience of showing the boy around, knowing he would be fascinated with the shipping on the river clearly visible from the large floor-to-ceiling windows that made up one entire wall of the apartment.

He was just clearing up after his supper, eaten while watching the sky darken and the lights of London come on on the far bank, when his phone rang. To his delight, on answering he found it was Jamie.

'Is it all right for the weekend?' he said, and Nathan could hear the anxiety in his voice.

'Yes, Jamie, it's fine,' he replied. 'There's so much I want to show you. I really didn't think it would be possible to get you down here so soon, but seeing that Mum and Martin are coming to London, it's a perfect opportunity.'

'So you don't have to work?'

'No, I don't,' said Nathan, silently thanking Richard for being so accommodating over the on-call roster for the weekend. 'I'm looking forward to showing you where I live and I thought perhaps a ride on the London Eye might be in order. What do you think?'

'That would be cool,' said Jamie. He spoke nonchalantly but Nathan could detect the excitement in his voice and he smiled.

'And on Sunday I've been told there is a fun day at the hospital. It's being held in the grounds and apparently there will be lots going on.'

'What sort of things?' asked Jamie doubtfully.

'Well, I suppose sideshows and games—and I guess there'll be lots of other children there. What do you think, would you like to go to that?'

'If you think it'll be all right.' Jamie still sounded dubious.

'Tell you what, we'll give it a try and if you don't like it, we won't stay too long—how's that?'

'Yes, OK,' said Jamie, and as Nathan detected the relief in his voice he felt a pang deep inside and not for the first time found himself worrying that his son seemed to have little contact with other children and was turning into a bit of a loner.

'I'd better go now, Dad,' said Jamie after a moment. 'I've got some homework to do.'

'All right, Jamie. Bye for now. Take care and I'll see you on Saturday!'

'Yes, see you Saturday!'

After he'd hung up, Nathan sat on for a while in the twilight but the slight melancholia he'd felt earlier had gone now, replaced by the joyful anticipation at the prospect of spending time with his son. Briefly he found himself wondering whether or not Olivia would be at the fun day with her children, then he dismissed the thought. For a moment there he'd hoped she would be, but it was better not to go down that road—alluring as Olivia Gilbert might be, she quite definitely was, and should remain, forbidden fruit.

CHAPTER FOUR

'GOOD morning, Olivia.'

'Good morning, Nathan.'

'I'm so pleased you are to be in on this one,' he said, with a smile.

'Where else would I be on such an important morning?' She spoke lightly but to her consternation she realised she was intensely aware of him as he came to stand beside her in the theatre scrub room.

'I thought you might have been off duty, or maybe one of your colleagues might have been scheduled for Theatre today.'

'I particularly requested to be present,' she said, as they began the rigorous scrubbing up procedure required before entering Theatre.

'Have you spoken to the parents this morning?' he asked after a moment.

'Yes,' she said, 'I slipped along to Special Care and had a word with them.'

'How were they?'

'Well, how you would expect really. But…' She paused reflectively. 'Actually surprisingly positive. One nice touch was that their other children had made cards and a banner for William, wishing him luck.'

Nathan smiled. 'Perhaps the banner should have been for me,' he said wryly.

She threw him a sidelong glance. 'You're confident, aren't you?'

'As confident as it's possible to be, but I'm always aware that in these situations complications can arise—especially when such a young baby is concerned.'

'That's true.' She rinsed the lather from her hands. 'But if we'd waited any longer, he would have stood no chance at all.'

'Just as long as the family are fully aware of the risks.'

'Oh, I would say so,' Olivia replied, then after a pause she added, 'So much so that baby William was baptised last evening.'

'Were you there?' he asked as he dried his hands.

'Yes, I stayed on at Julie and Dave's request and I stood in as godmother for one of their relatives.'

'That's nice. I think we sometimes lose sight of just how close we can be regarded by the families of our patients. And I would say that is especially true when the patients are children.'

'Or babies,' agreed Olivia, as she finished drying her hands and together they made their way into Theatre. Baby William, lying on a specially warmed mattress, was already in the capable hands of Diana, the anaesthetist, and Theatre Sister Elizabeth Saunders. They both looked up as Nathan and Olivia approached.

'Just look at him,' said Diana in her gruff, hearty manner. 'He's a cracking little lad, isn't he?'

The others agreed and after Olivia had carried out a final examination on the baby, the theatre sister covered him with drapes, just leaving his chest area exposed for the cardiac team, headed by Nathan, to move in.

During the delicate and highly complicated procedure to close the hole in the baby's heart, Olivia stood back, observing the operation step by step on the monitor screens at the rear of the theatre.

More than once she found herself watching Nathan, his movements, his body language and the way he interacted with the rest of the team. There was something about him that fascinated her—no, more than that, mesmerised her if she was really honest. She liked his style, the way he included everyone in Theatre in what was happening, the way he was able to talk of other, everyday things in spite of the highly charged tension of the work they were doing, recognising that in this way he created an atmosphere not of sloppiness but of relaxation which would bring out the best in his team. He liked music playing as well—light classical music, which everyone seemed to know. Some surgeons preferred working in absolute silence while others indulged in heavy rock or house music, often to the exasperation of other team members who would invariably leave the theatre tense and irritated.

Several times her gaze flickered from the screen to Nathan then to the tiny, still mound on the table while inside her heart went out to the couple who waited outside in the recovery room for news of their baby son. She knew how she would feel if it were Charlotte or Lewis and their lives hanging in the balance.

There was a moment of high drama about an hour into the operation when baby William's blood pressure suddenly dropped and Diana called for the operation to halt. Plainly frustrated, Nathan stood back while the team struggled to stabilise the baby, then when Diana gave the all-clear Olivia stepped forward, examined him again then indicated to Nathan that it was safe to continue.

At last it was over, with Nathan himself closing the incision instead of delegating the task to his assistant, which would normally have been the case.

'Right,' said Olivia. 'Let's get this little lad into Recovery.' Gently she lifted him from the table into his incubator then, glancing up at Nathan, she said, 'Do you want to come to Recovery with me to see the parents?'

'Yes, of course,' he replied, removing the large plastic apron that covered his scrubs then pulling off his mask. Olivia did likewise, also taking off her theatre cap and shaking out her hair. Together with Elizabeth Saunders, who guided the incubator, they walked into the recovery room where they found Dave and Julie. Julie was sitting in a wheelchair and Dave was staring out of the room's only window. They both swung round as the others entered.

'Is he all right?' Julie's gaze flew to the incubator. 'How did it go?'

It was Nathan who answered. 'It went well,' he said. 'I've closed the hole, William is stabilised and as far as I'm concerned the operation was completely successful.'

'Oh, thank you. Thank you.' Julie was almost sobbing in her relief while Dave, who Olivia noticed had several days' stubble on his jaw and looked as if he hadn't slept since William's birth, seemed to visibly slump as Nathan finished speaking. Together they turned towards the incubator and moved forward to see their son, reaching out their hands to touch the plastic case that enfolded him. Then baby William was wheeled away so that he could be closely monitored.

'What happens next?' asked Dave shakily.

'Once the staff here are satisfied, he will be taken back to the high-dependency wing of the special care unit,' Olivia replied. 'I would expect him to be there for two or three days then if all goes well he will come out of High Dependency but remain in Special Care for the time being.'

'Can I go and ring the family?' asked Dave eagerly. 'They'll all be waiting and wanting to know.'

'Of course,' said Nathan. 'So would I if I were in their shoes.'

'Right, we'll do that together, then, Julie,' he said to his wife. He turned back to Nathan. 'Oh, and, Mr Carrington, thank you again—we cannot begin to tell you how grateful we are. And to you, too, Dr Gilbert.'

'There's one happy little family,' observed Nathan as together with Olivia he left the recovery room and they headed towards the theatre showers. 'It's humbling to think what responsibility we bear.'

'I understand you have a son,' said Olivia. She found herself holding her breath as she waited for his reply, but didn't know quite why that should be.

'That's right.' He sounded faintly surprised that she should know. 'His name is Jamie.'

'And how old is Jamie?' she asked.

'He's eight,' he replied. He paused. 'You also have children, I believe?' he added after a moment.

'Yes, I do,' she agreed. 'Charlotte is seven and Lewis is five.'

'So we know just how those parents must be feeling, and countless others like them,' said Nathan. 'I really don't know what I would be like if it was Jamie facing life-threatening surgery.'

'Probably better than if he had a life-threatening condition and surgery wasn't possible,' Olivia replied.

'That's true,' he agreed. 'But it must be agony, whatever the circumstances.'

'Talking of that,' said Olivia, 'do we have a date yet for Sara Middleton's surgery?'

'I saw on the planner this morning that she has been pencilled in for early next week—possibly Monday or Tuesday, but we'll confirm that with you as soon as we know.'

'Thank you.' She smiled. 'That will be a traumatic day for Sara's family—her mother especially. They've waited so long for the conditions to be right for this. I only hope nothing happens to jeopardise it in the meantime.'

He went then into the showers and for the briefest of moments Olivia found herself wishing that she could get to know him better. She dismissed the thought almost before it had formed. She didn't want to get to know anyone better, didn't want any situation that might lead to any sort of involvement. That was something she was perfectly clear about and, besides, even if she did, there wouldn't be any point getting to know Nathan better because he was married—a married man with a family. And yet... Deep inside she felt a pang. It had been a long time since she'd been married and if she was perfectly honest she desperately missed the closeness, the intimacy of sharing her life with someone. It seemed, these days, that everywhere she went there were couples, everyone she met was part of a couple. She felt so alone at times, like a stranger looking in on some celebration from which she was excluded. But she wasn't at all sure she wanted it any other way. To do so would mean letting someone through that hard shell she'd built around herself and, really, that was the last thing she wanted.

Once back in the children's ward, Kirstin asked her how the operation had gone.

'Pretty well,' Olivia said. 'There was one tense moment when the baby's blood pressure dropped rather alarmingly, but we stabilised him and the surgical team were able to carry on.'

'Was it Richard Parker?' asked Kirstin.

'No, Nathan Carrington,' Olivia replied. For some obscure reason as she said his name she felt her cheeks grow warm, which really was absolutely ridiculous. Quickly she turned away and busied herself with sorting through some notes, hoping desperately that Kirstin wouldn't notice her discomfort. She knew that her friend would seize upon it and misconstrue it.

'Nathan Carrington, eh?' Kirstin may not have noticed her reaction but it seemed she wasn't prepared to let the subject drop. 'So what's he like in Theatre?'

'Good,' Olivia admitted, casually, she hoped. 'I liked his style,' she added, 'relaxed and a bit laid back but very much in control of his team.'

'Music?' Kirstin raised one eyebrow.

'Yes.' Olivia nodded.

'Let me guess. Jazz, I would say.'

'Would you believe heavy metal?'

'No, I wouldn't.'

'You're right.' Olivia chuckled. 'Light classics, actually, which had everyone humming along.'

'Clever man,' said Kirstin. 'Brains, looks and common sense—deadly combination, that. Pity he's spoken for.'

Yes, Olivia thought, it is.

Nathan's intercom buzzed at ten-thirty on Saturday morning. 'Hello?' he said.

'Dad, it's me—Jamie.'

'Come on up, Jamie.'

Moments later he opened the door of his apartment to find Jamie on the landing with his mother. The boy hurled himself at him and hugged him fiercely. Nathan felt the breath catch in his throat and hugged him back with equal intensity, then he looked up at the dark-haired woman who stood back slightly, holding Jamie's rucksack. 'Hello, Susan,' he said, faintly surprised that for once the sight of her didn't seem to affect him as it had done so many other times since they'd parted.

'Hello, Nathan. He has everything he needs,' she went on quickly, not really allowing time for further conversation, instead handing over the rucksack. 'If you should need to contact us, we're staying at the Savoy. Otherwise, I'll ring you tonight, Jamie, then we'll pick you up tomorrow at five o'clock.'

'Five o'clock?' Nathan frowned.

'Is there a problem with that?' Susan's voice took on a defensive note and she raised her eyebrows.

'No, not really.' Nathan shrugged. 'It's just that we're going to a fun day at the hospital but I dare say it'll all be over by then.'

'We need to be away by five if we are to get home at a reasonable time.'

'Yes, of course—that's fine,' said Nathan as he saw Jamie's expression change to one of anxiety. 'We'll be back by then.' He paused. 'Do you want to come in? A drink or something?'

'No, we won't stop. Martin's outside in the car.' She bent down and kissed Jamie. 'Bye, Jamie,' she said. 'See you tomorrow.'

'Bye, Mum,' he said.

Then Susan was gone, her high heels clicking on the wooden floor as she made her way to the lift.

'Right, then,' said Nathan as he closed the door. 'We'd better get this show on the road. London Eye this morning, lunch at McDonald's then I thought perhaps the London Dungeons this afternoon—what do you think?'

'Cool,' said Jamie.

'But first come and give me another hug.'

'Come on,' said Olivia as she held the car door open. 'Hurry up or we'll be late.'

'I wanted to take Daphne,' grumbled Lewis, as he scrambled into the back of the car and Olivia checked that both he and Charlotte had fastened their seat belts.

'I know you did,' said Olivia, 'but I really don't think this is the right place for a gerbil.'

'There's a barbeque, isn't there?' said Charlotte, and when her mother nodded in agreement she went on, 'They might have put her in a roll—like a hot dog.'

'They don't use real dogs, do they?' whispered Lewis.

Olivia glanced in her driving mirror, saw her son's eyes were like saucers and hastened to reassure him.

After they'd arrived at the hospital and parked the car, Olivia led the way to the spacious grounds at the rear of the main buildings, where they found that the proceedings were in full swing. Many stalls and sideshows had been erected around the grounds; the barbeque had been set up at one end and in another corner a large bouncy castle had been erected. Charlotte and Lewis were soon rounded up by Kirstin's three children and borne away to join in the fun.

'I'm so glad you came,' said Kirstin. 'And my kids were pleased that Charlotte and Lewis were coming.'

'Yes, I'm glad we came,' said Olivia, as she took the glass

of fruit cup that Kirstin poured for her. 'Looks like nearly all the staff who have children are here.'

'Yes, Kirstin agreed. 'It's good that some of the patients can join in as well.'

Olivia turned and saw that several children from the ward, those who were well enough, were sitting on the balcony or on the grass under the trees. Even Sara, seated in a wheelchair and wearing a pink baseball cap, was there with her mother and her brother and sister.

'The Lathwell-Foxes are here with their children too,' said Kirstin.

'Claudia and Rory? Really? That's nice.' As Kirstin was distracted by some newcomers, Olivia looked around to see if she could see Claudia, but as she scanned the crowd it gradually dawned on her that in fact it wasn't really Claudia she was looking for but Nathan.

But she couldn't see him and was about to move away to find somewhere to sit when a voice at her elbow stopped her in her tracks.

'Olivia, I wondered if you'd be here.'

She turned sharply, almost spilling her drink to find him right beside her. 'Sorry,' he said. 'I startled you. You were looking for someone.'

'Oh,' she said. 'Oh, yes… I was looking for—Claudia,' she added hurriedly, not wanting for one moment for him to suspect she'd been looking for him.

'Claudia? She's here, is she? And Rory?' He, too, began looking around scanning the crowd of people in the grounds.

'Apparently, yes. I didn't know Claudia was coming, but Kirstin said they were both here with the children. And, of course, I'd forgotten—Rory's on the committee this year.'

She paused then before he could say anything further, she went on, 'I guess practically all the staff are here, especially those with children.'

'True,' Nathan agreed, then after a moment he said, 'Your children—are they here?'

'Oh, yes.' Olivia nodded. 'They're over there on the bouncy castle.' As he turned to look, she added, 'That's Charlotte with the striped top and Lewis—you can't mistake Lewis, he's the one with the mop of black curls.' She paused then threw a tentative glance in his direction. He looked relaxed and carefree in faded jeans and a white T-shirt and ever so slightly she felt her pulse quicken. In an effort to quell it she said, 'And your son, is he here?'

'Yes, that's Jamie over there.' He indicated a boy who stood a little apart from the other children, watching them as if he was uncertain whether or not to join in. He was a dark-haired boy who, just by his stance and even from the distance that separated them, Olivia would have known was Nathan's son.

'He looks like you,' she observed.

'So people tell me,' said Nathan. He spoke casually but Olivia suspected that he was pleased that she had said so. 'He has his mother's eyes, however.'

Olivia took a deep breath but in the same casual tone she'd endeavoured to adopt ever since he had appeared, she said, 'And she's here, is she?'

'I'm sorry?' He half turned towards her and frowned.

'Jamie's mother,' she said. 'Is she here?'

'Lord, no,' he replied, and there was something in the way he said it which caused Olivia to turn and look at him in surprise.

'She dropped Jamie off for the weekend—she's picking him up again later this afternoon.' He took a mouthful of his drink then something in Olivia's face must have made him realise that further explanation was required. 'Jamie's mother and I are divorced,' he said.

'Oh,' she said, 'I see.' Somewhere deep inside she was aware of a pang at his words, a pang that seemed to trigger a warning bell in her brain.

'Jamie lives with his mother and her partner in Chester.'

'Do you get to see much of him?' she asked.

'As much as I can,' he replied, his expression now holding a hint of sadness, 'but I have to admit that's not as much as I would like, and I fear that now I'm in London that may be even less than when I was living in Oxford. I have to say this weekend is a rare treat for us both—his mother and her partner had to come down to London for the weekend.'

Together, as if by some unspoken agreement, they began to stroll around the stalls. There were games and sideshows— a coconut shy, hoopla, skittles and a rifle range. The June sunshine was warm on their backs and shoulders and gradually in the easy pleasant atmosphere Olivia felt herself relax.

'Dad.' Suddenly Jamie was at Nathan's elbow. 'Someone has just said the food's ready.'

'Is it, now?' Nathan laughed, his easy, ready laugh. 'In that case, we'd better go and get some. But first, Jamie, I'd like you to meet Dr Gilbert.'

'Hello, Jamie.' She shook hands with the boy, who remarkably looked even more like his father at closer quarters but whose eyes, instead of being green, were brown. 'I'm very pleased to meet you. I'll come with you, if I may, to get some food, and on the way we'll collect my two children.'

Together they moved away in the direction of the bouncy

castle, where Olivia beckoned to Charlotte and Lewis to join them.

'We're having fun,' Charlotte complained.

'Don't you want some food?' asked Olivia.

'I do,' said Lewis.

'I thought you would,' said Olivia with a laugh. She turned to Jamie. 'Jamie, this is Charlotte and this is Lewis. Now, you two, this is Jamie and this is his father, Mr Carrington.'

'Hi, Jamie,' said Charlotte and Lewis in unison. 'Hello, Mr Carrington.'

'Hello,' said Jamie shyly, while Nathan solemnly shook hands with Charlotte and Lewis.

'Take Jamie with you and collect your plates and cutlery,' said Olivia, 'then take your place in the queue for food.'

'What about you, Dad?' said Jamie anxiously.

'Don't worry,' said Nathan. 'We'll be right behind you. Isn't that right, Olivia?'

'Too right,' Olivia agreed with a laugh.

'Thanks for that,' said Nathan quietly as the children ran on ahead. 'Jamie can be rather shy, especially around children he doesn't know.'

'My two won't give him a chance to be shy,' said Olivia. 'Charlotte will take him under her wing—a born mother hen that one—and Lewis will look up to him just as if he's a big brother—you wait and see.'

They ate together around one of the wooden picnic tables that had been especially set up for the day—a striped parasol shielding them from the noonday sun. The food was delicious—succulent chicken joints, juicy steaks, sausages and burgers and great bowls of mixed salads served with crusty French loaves and baked potatoes. The children seemed to get on really well and it was while Nathan, Charlotte and Jamie had gone to collect puddings for them all that Kirstin suddenly appeared and perched beside Olivia on the bench. 'Now, this,' she said, 'is what I call a barbeque. I've just said to Malc, in future I shall expect the same standard.'

'And what did he say to that?' said Olivia with a smile.

'I won't repeat it—not in front of Lewis,' said Kirstin with a sniff. With a glance over her shoulder, she said, 'I was looking for you just now but you were otherwise engaged.'

'I don't know what you mean,' said Olivia lightly, but she smiled nevertheless. Suddenly she found she really didn't care what anyone thought. She was simply enjoying the day and, yes, if she was really honest she was also enjoying Nathan's company.

'Oh,' said Kirstin, 'I think you do, and I have to say I don't blame you one little bit. I think he's absolutely gorgeous and it's high time you had a bit of fun.'

'Kirstin, let's not get carried away here. This is just a pleasant day out, that's all…'

'Maybe, but do you know what I heard?' Kirstin leaned forward then glanced over her shoulder to make sure no one was in earshot.

'No, Kirstin, I don't know what you heard,' said Olivia, 'but I don't doubt you are about to tell me.'

Undaunted, Kirstin carried straight on, 'You know we thought he was married? Well, he isn't,' she went on, without giving Olivia time to comment. 'At least, he was, but he's divorced now so that rather puts a whole new slant on things, doesn't it?'

'I don't know what you mean,' said Olivia with a little shrug.

'You know exactly what I mean,' said Kirstin bluntly. 'He's

.

free, Olivia. He's gorgeous and it's blatantly obvious he's more than interested in you.'

'I can't imagine where you got that idea.' Olivia shot a look at Lewis, wondering what he was making of this particular conversation, but to her relief he didn't appear to even be listening. Instead, he was deeply engrossed in the progress of a pair of ladybirds, which were crawling along one edge of the picnic table. 'And besides,' she went on, 'even if it were true, which I very much doubt, as I've told you many times before, Kirstin, I'm simply not interested.'

'I know, I know that's what you've said,' said Kirstin, holding up her hands defensively, 'but honestly, Olivia, I'm sure…' But that was as far as she got for at that moment Nathan and the children returned, laden with a mouth-watering selection of puddings. Olivia knew Kirstin had been about to bring Marcus's name into it and she was grateful for the interruption. She'd already had tears from Charlotte that morning over Father's Day and she didn't want the children reminded of Marcus any more than was necessary. Kirstin meant well, she knew that…but Kirstin only knew half the story.

'We've brought a bit of everything,' said Nathan with a laugh. 'Cheesecake, gateau, trifle and, oh, yes, chocolate profiteroles. Oh, hello, Kirstin,' he added. 'Sorry, didn't see you there.'

'That's OK. I was just having a chat with Olivia. I'm in your seat, Nathan. I'll move.'

'No, please, don't move on my account,' he said, setting down the dishes and looking around. 'I'll fetch another chair.'

'No.' Kirstin scrambled to her feet. 'I must get back to Malc and the kids—they'll wonder where I am. But I must say those puds look absolutely delicious. I think I'll collect a few on the way back, and blow the diet. See you guys later.' With a wave of her hand she was gone.

They tucked into the puddings then later, after the children had disappeared again in the direction of the bouncy castle, they moved into the shade of a mulberry tree and sat together contentedly, talking. It occurred to Olivia how easy it was to talk to Nathan, how down to earth he was and lacking in any sense of pretence. He told her about his training days—the hospitals he'd worked in—and had just reached the point where he had drawn the conversation round to herself and was asking about her medical training when suddenly Rory appeared before them.

'Sorry, Olivia,' he said, glancing at her, 'but, Nathan, we have a bit of a problem.'

'Oh? Anything I can help with?' Nathan looked up, shading his eyes from the glare of the sun with his hand.

'I hope so. The entertainer the committee had hired to amuse the children has just phoned to say he's broken down on the North Circular—he's never going to make it on time.'

'What was he going to do?' asked Nathan.

'Magic, conjuring, that sort of thing,' Rory replied.

'Well, I hope you're not expecting me to—'

'No, of course not—but I feel we have to do something for the kids. That castle is beginning to lose its appeal and, really, it was only for the younger ones anyway. No, I was wondering…'

'I know what you're thinking,' said Nathan, hauling himself to his feet.

'What's that?' said Olivia, looking from one to the other.

'Treasure hunt,' said Nathan.

'Great standby for keeping kids entertained—and adults,

too, for that matter,' said Rory. 'I'll go and get some prizes then we'll see if we can get them hidden without anyone noticing.'

Within half an hour Rory and Nathan had set up the treasure hunt and very soon all the children were involved in the search. At one point Olivia saw Nathan cross the grass to Sara and her family, and a moment later he was pushing the girl in her wheelchair around the trees while Sara squealed with delight. And a little later Olivia was certain she wasn't the only one to have a lump in her throat when, not surprisingly, they returned, with Sara triumphantly waving a box of sweets in the air, her face flushed and beaming with joy.

When all the treasure had been found, Olivia and Nathan took Charlotte, Lewis and Jamie on a tour of the stalls. Charlotte won a toy penguin on the hoopla stall, Jamie a tin of toffees on the coconut shy, and when Nathan won a tiger on the rifle range, he promptly gave it to Lewis.

Olivia couldn't remember when she had last enjoyed anything quite so much, and it had certainly done her good to see Charlotte and Lewis so happy. It had been a tough time for them all over the last two years and happiness and laughter had been in pretty short supply, but it seemed that summer's afternoon in the grounds of St Benedict's something had happened. She wasn't quite certain what that something was. She could only hope that it might herald the beginning of a new phase, if not exactly in her life—for she still wasn't sure that she was ready for anything as drastic as that—at least for the children.

Later, as she sat beneath the welcome shade of the mulberry tree once again and sipped a cool drink, she found her gaze drawn to Nathan as he played skittles with the children. She'd laughingly dismissed Kirstin's suggestions that he was interested in her but she had to admit she really had felt something when she'd realised that he was unattached. And as she watched him she found herself wondering about his marriage and why it had failed. What sort of woman was it who could walk away from a man like Nathan Carrington? Or had it been the other way round—had he walked away from her? Had she been unfaithful—or had he? Was he the sort of man who could cheat on a woman behind her back? Her hands tightened on her glass. Would she be storing up all sorts of trouble if she allowed herself to get to know him better? But surely, she admonished herself, she was rushing ahead here for, in spite of Kirstin's wishful thinking, there was no real indication that Nathan wanted any sort of relationship between them other than a purely professional one.

The afternoon drifted on in a warm haze of gossip and laughter as first Claudia came over to chat and then some other colleagues, and almost before she knew it Nathan was standing before her, saying he and Jamie would have to go.

'Do we have to?' said Jamie. He looked hot and flushed but very happy, far happier than the rather uncertain little boy who had stood on the fringes of the crowd earlier, watching the other children.

'Yes, Jamie, I'm afraid we do.' Even Nathan sounded reluctant as if he, too, didn't want the day to end. 'Your mum will be arriving to collect you and we have to get through the traffic yet.'

'Can I come down again and see everyone?' asked Jamie.

'Of course you can,' said Charlotte. 'Can't he, Mum?'

'Yes, I'm sure something can be arranged,' murmured Olivia. Suddenly she found it impossible to look at Nathan.

'There you are,' said Nathan, 'something to look forward

to. Now, come on, Jamie, let's go and say some goodbyes.' He paused then with an almost shy glance at Olivia he said, 'Goodbye, Olivia, see you tomorrow.'

'Yes,' she said. 'See you tomorrow.'

They watched Nathan and Jamie walk away then with a little sigh Olivia stood up. 'I suppose we should be thinking about going as well,' she said to Charlotte and Lewis. Together they began to trail back across the grounds where the crowd was thinning out now and the children from Paediatrics were being taken back to their wards.

'I've had a lovely time,' said Charlotte with a deep sigh.

'That's good.' Olivia put one arm around her daughter. 'And what about you?' she asked, resting her other arm around Lewis and drawing him closer. 'Have you had a good time as well?'

'Yes,' he said, 'but one thing, Mum…'

'Yes, darling…sorry, Lewis,' she corrected herself. 'What's that?'

'What does being divorced mean?' he asked earnestly.

CHAPTER FIVE

'DID you enjoy that?' Nathan cast a sideways glance at his son as he sat beside him in the front seat of the car, his baseball cap pulled down over his eyes.

'Yeah, it was cool,' Jamie said.

'I thought you would.' Nathan smiled. 'It was nice for you to be able to spend some time with other children.'

'Lewis is all right,' said Jamie after a while.

'What about Charlotte?'

'Yeah, she's OK.' He wriggled down further in his seat. 'For a girl,' he added. He was silent for a while as Nathan negotiated a particularly busy roundabout then slowly he said, 'I feel sorry for them, actually.'

'Who?'

'Charlie and Lewis.'

'Charlie? I thought her name was Charlotte.'

'It is, but she told me she likes to be called Charlie. Her mum calls her Charlotte, though.'

'I see. Why do you feel sorry for them?' Nathan was suddenly curious.

'Because it was Father's Day and they don't have a dad.'

For some reason, Nathan found he was gripping the

steering-wheel a little bit more tightly than usual. 'You mean their parents are divorced?' he said. He spoke casually but was aware that his heart had started to thump as he waited for his son's answer.

'No.' Jamie shook his head. 'Their dad's dead.'

'Dead?' Nathan shot a startled glance in Jamie's direction. 'What happened? Was he ill or something?'

'No, Charlie said he was killed in a car crash. She was going to tell me about it but she started to cry.'

Nathan drew his breath in sharply. 'That's very sad, Jamie,' he said. 'I know you don't get to see me as often as either you or I would like, but at least I'm still around.'

Jamie nodded. 'I'd hate it if you died, Dad,' he said.

'Well, I haven't got any plans to do that,' said Nathan, trying to make light of the matter, 'so if I were you, I wouldn't worry about it.'

'Charlie's dad didn't know he was going to die either,' said Jamie after a while. 'Charlie said he just went out and… he didn't come home.'

'Well, unfortunately accidents do happen sometimes,' Nathan agreed, 'but none of us should go through life expecting the worst to happen, because more often than not it doesn't.'

'But it did for Charlie and Lewis,' said Jamie.

'Yes,' Nathan was forced to agree, 'it did for them.'

Jamie was silent after that until they reached Nathan's apartment and then there was only time for him to have a quick drink and a sandwich and pack his rucksack before a ring on the doorbell heralded the arrival of his mother.

'We can't stop,' she told Nathan. 'Martin wants to get away before the traffic builds up.'

He hadn't the heart or the inclination to point out that the bulk of the Sunday evening traffic would be pouring back into the capital and not out of it. Deep down he suspected that Susan's real reason for not coming into his apartment had nothing to do with traffic.

'Have you had a good time?' The question, aimed at Jamie, was a perfunctory one.

'Brilliant.' His reply was far from perfunctory and seemed to take Susan aback. 'It was cool,' he added, 'and we had a treasure hunt, didn't we, Dad?'

'We did indeed,' Nathan agreed. Briefly his eyes met Susan's and he knew she was thinking of other occasions in the past, when they'd been together, in what had been something of a tradition when families and friends had joined forces in hilarious and often frantic treasure hunts.

'Well, that was nice,' she said, then, almost as if she didn't know quite what else to say in the face of such enthusiasm, she went on, 'We'd better go, Jamie. Say goodbye to your dad.'

As Nathan hugged Jamie, bade him a fond farewell and watched him and Susan walk away from the apartment and into the lift, it hit him once again that this time seeing Susan really hadn't affected him.

Slowly he walked back into his apartment, closed the door behind him and briefly leaned against it. It always affected him, saying goodbye to Jamie, and he knew that whatever the circumstances might be in the future it would continue to do so. But where Susan was concerned it was another matter. He'd always known that while she was still able to affect him, there was little likelihood that he would be able to move on and place his trust in someone else. But this weekend, for some reason, had been different...

It had surprised—no shocked—him really when Jamie had

told him that Charlotte and Lewis had lost their father in an accident. For a time he'd simply imagined that Olivia's husband was absent for some explainable reason, then briefly he had wondered if, like him, she was divorced. It hadn't occurred to him that she might be a widow. For some reason, it seemed to put a whole new perspective on the situation. For a start, she was single, unattached, and while being a widow also seemed to make her appear more vulnerable, that very vulnerability in itself caused his pulse to race a little faster than usual.

She had looked especially lovely that day in a long, floral skirt and a white top with tiny straps, which had showed off her smooth back and a smattering of freckles across her tanned shoulders. That glorious black hair had for the most part been hidden under a straw hat, only escaping during the treasure hunt when she had discarded the hat and shaken her hair loose so that it fell on her shoulders.

Her children had been lovely, too, Charlotte with her coltish long limbs and tangle of blonde hair and Lewis with his mother's dark eyes and hair. Jamie had liked them, wanted to see them again…

With a sigh he pushed himself away from the door and walked back into his sitting room. The Father's Day card that Jamie had given him stood on the mantelpiece, together with his present, a DVD of a new sci-fi adventure which they had watched and enjoyed together over a take-away the night before.

He was restless and found he couldn't settle to anything, instead prowling the apartment like some caged animal. He wanted to talk to her, to tell her that he knew about her late husband, that he sympathised with her. He wanted to tell her about himself, his own situation, about how his divorce had come about, how it had devastated him and left him bitter and distrusting.

But he could hardly just turn up on her doorstep—she would think he was mad, especially after they'd just spent the best part of the day in each other's company.

Maybe he could phone her. Yes, that was it! He brightened at the thought but then he was faced with the problem of why he was phoning. What on earth could he say? Could he simply say he was calling to make sure she'd got home safely? No, that was pretty ridiculous. She'd only had a few miles to go— it wasn't as if she'd had to travel a vast distance on motorways. Could he ask her something about work? He racked his brain but couldn't come up with a plausible excuse, something that couldn't wait until the next morning. And maybe—that was it—he would be seeing her the next day at work, and while there wouldn't exactly be opportunity to discuss the sort of things he had in mind, it would quite simply have to suffice.

There was a definite feeling of anti-climax when Olivia arrived home with the children. Apart from Oscar's habitual thumping welcome, the house seemed empty and very quiet as Helene had gone to spend the day with some friends.

'I've had a lovely time,' declared Charlotte as she pulled off her sunhat, the one with the huge sunflower on the front of its upturned brim. 'I wish Jamie didn't live in Chester.'

'I know,' Olivia agreed, as she set about feeding Oscar. 'It is rather a long way away.'

'Do you think we could go and see him?' demanded Charlotte.

'I don't really think that would be possible,' said Olivia slowly. 'Jamie lives with his mum and her new partner, you see.'

'Yes, I know all that,' said Charlotte with a sigh, 'but I didn't say everything I wanted to say—there wasn't time.'

Olivia knew exactly what Charlotte meant because she, too, was feeling that her conversation with Nathan had been cut short. She knew she would see him at work but somehow that wasn't quite the same. Somehow she couldn't quite imagine talking about personal things in the middle of tricky heart surgery.

No, there was no doubt about it—the day had suddenly gone very flat. She wondered if she could perhaps phone Nathan, tell him how much they had enjoyed themselves and maybe arrange something for the next time that Jamie came to London. But, surely, if she did that he would think she was mad and, besides, she really did need to be careful—there was no telling where this sort of thing could lead given even a scrap of encouragement. And she didn't want that, did she?

Of course not, she told herself firmly. Nothing like that at all... But, still, it would have been nice just to talk to him... discuss the day they had shared.

For the next half-hour or so she tried to put all such thoughts out of her mind as she prepared the children's clothes and homework for school the following day, and she had just resigned herself to yet another lonely evening on her own when a sudden shout from Lewis changed everything.

'Mu-um!'

Olivia went into the hall and found him sitting on the top stair. 'What is it?' she said.

'Look what I've just found in my pocket,' he said, and held up a pair of sunglasses. 'They're Jamie's,' he added, when Olivia frowned.

'What are you doing with them?' she asked.

'He let me wear them,' Lewis replied. 'Then when we went on the treasure hunt I put them in my pocket so they wouldn't get broken. I forgot to give them back to him.'

'Do you think he will have gone home yet?' said Charlotte, who suddenly appeared on the landing and joined Lewis on the top stair.

'I don't know, but I would have thought so,' said Olivia slowly. 'And really we can't do anything about them today anyway—I don't even have Mr Carrington's telephone number.'

'I do,' said Charlotte triumphantly.

'You do?' Olivia stared up at her daughter. 'What on earth do you have it for?'

'I gave Jamie our number and our address and he gave me his number in Chester and his dad's number here in London.'

'Oh…right.' Olivia was rather taken aback but at the same time was aware of a little stab of excitement in that she now had a legitimate reason to phone Nathan. 'Well, in that case, I'd better give him a ring,' she said.

'I'll do it,' said Charlotte loftily.

'No, I think in the circumstances it would be better if I did it,' Olivia replied firmly.

'Oh, all right.' Charlotte pouted a bit but duly went off and came back with the number. Olivia walked into the kitchen and with the children at her heels picked up the phone. With a hand that trembled slightly, she pressed out the digits of the number. She could hear the phone ringing and for one wild moment she wondered what she was going to say. Then, suddenly, Nathan answered. At the sound of his voice her heart lurched.

'Oh,' she said. 'Is that Nathan?'

'Yes.' His voice sounded guarded—or was it expectant?

'Nathan, it's Olivia.' She paused slightly and could have sworn she heard him catch his breath. 'I'm sorry to bother you, but is Jamie still with you?'

'No, Olivia, I'm sorry, he left about an hour ago.'

'Oh, I see. He's gone already.' She pulled a face at the children, who both promptly lost interest in the whole thing and disappeared back upstairs. 'It's just that Lewis has come home with Jamie's sunglasses in the pocket of his shorts.'

'Oh, never mind...' Nathan began.

'I think Lewis is worried about it, and I have to say they do look a rather nice pair of sunglasses.'

'Yes,' said Nathan, cryptically, she thought, 'they would be. But, like I say, don't worry about it.'

'So I'll bring them to work, shall I?'

'Yes, OK, if you would.'

'Anyway, I'm sorry to have disturbed you...'

'Not at all—you're not disturbing anything. If I'm honest, I'm feeling at a bit of a loose end after all the excitement of today.'

'That's funny,' said Olivia. 'So am I. I was just thinking it seems a real anti-climax now that it's all over.'

'It was a great day, wasn't it?'

'Yes,' she agreed, 'it was.' She hesitated then from somewhere she heard herself say, 'Listen, if you aren't doing anything, would you like to come over for a bite of supper?'

'I'd love to,' he said. 'That is,' he added hastily, 'if you're sure.'

'Yes, of course I'm sure. It will round off the day nicely.'

After she'd given him her address and instructions on the quickest way to reach it, she hung up and sat for a moment, staring at the phone. What had she done? She could scarcely believe it. She'd actually invited him over to supper. She took a deep breath. But where was the big deal in that, for heaven's sake? In the old days she wouldn't have thought twice about inviting half a dozen people to supper just on the spur of the moment. But that had been then, when Marcus had been alive, and this was now and she was on her own. She couldn't remember that she'd actually done any entertaining since Marcus had died, with the exception of his mother Grace who came to stay from time to time, and her own parents on their annual visit from their home in Provence. Some of her friends popped in occasionally for coffee or a drink and a sandwich, but that wasn't real entertaining, and really, she told herself firmly, neither was this—it was, quite simply, supper between two people who had spent a pleasant day in the company of their children, their friends and each other. Nothing more could be read into it whatsoever.

So, if that was the case, why, as she began to raid the fridge to see what they could eat, did she find that her heart was thumping with barely concealed excitement?

Nathan could hardly believe it. There he'd been, desperately trying to concoct a reason to contact Olivia, and right out of the blue she'd phoned him. And if that hadn't been enough, what had started out to be a simple call to say that they had Jamie's sunglasses had turned into an invitation to supper.

He took a hasty shower and changed his clothes, snatched a bottle of red wine from the kitchen and hurried down to his car.

He found her house without any trouble from the instructions she'd given him and parked on the small forecourt beside her car. The house, situated in a quiet, tree-lined avenue, was a large, red-brick, three-storey Edwardian building, its gables and front door painted white and with a profusion of flowering shrubs in the borders around the forecourt. For some obscure reason, as Nathan rang the doorbell he felt nervous, as nervous as any gauche teenager on his first visit to meet his girlfriend's parents, which was quite ridiculous because this situation was nothing like that. This situation, quite purely and simply, was two colleagues, or friends even, meeting up to round off a rather pleasant day. There was no reason for him to think otherwise and certainly no reason to feel concerned that Olivia would read more into it. He wanted no more than that and most probably neither did she.

So, if that was the case, why, as he stood on her doorstep, waiting for someone to answer the door, did he find that his pulse was racing a lot faster than usual?

At last the door opened and he turned to face her, only to find that it wasn't Olivia who stood there but Charlotte. 'Hello again,' he said with a grin.

'Hello,' she said. 'Mum said you were coming to supper.'

'That's right.' He nodded.

'Mum!' she called. 'Mr Carrington's here!'

'Well, ask him in, then…' He heard Olivia's voice in the hallway behind Charlotte and then suddenly she was there and once again he found the breath caught in his throat. She'd also changed, out of the skirt and top she'd worn to the barbeque and into a pair of close-fitting black trousers and a white shirt in some soft, silky fabric, while that lovely black hair she'd tied back—just like she did at work—and fastened with a black bow at the nape of her neck. Behind her an elderly black Labrador ambled into the hall, sniffed the air and barked once.

'Sorry,' she said. 'Please, Nathan, do come in. Oscar, back in your bed, please.'

She thanked him for the bottle of wine he handed to her, then led him through the spacious hallway past various rooms that offered intriguing glimpses into what appeared to be a sitting room, a family room and possibly a study then into a large kitchen, which, with its long central table, Aga, and a dresser filled with willow-patterned china, was quite obviously the hub of the household. One wall was covered with the children's paintings and a large, cork notice-board smothered in various messages, notes, photographs and postcards, the paraphernalia of busy family life, all of which gave him a sudden pang as he thought of just how much he'd missed of Jamie's growing up.

To one side of the room a door opened into what seemed to be a small den where the dog, Oscar, was happily ensconced in his bed, while at the far end of the kitchen, double doors opened into a sun lounge. Beyond that, through a flower-laden pergola, Nathan caught a glimpse of a garden—lawns, trees and shrubs surrounded by a red brick wall.

'I thought,' said Olivia, 'that we'd eat in here. It's pleasant here because this side of the house catches the last of the evening sun.'

'It's a lovely house,' he said, crossing the quarry-tiled floor and looking out through the sun lounge and onto the patio beneath the pergola, packed with tubs of flowers. 'You obviously enjoy gardening.'

'I do, yes,' Olivia replied, 'but I have to have help with it these days. I simply don't have the time to keep it up. Just as I wouldn't be able to cope with the house and the children and my job if it wasn't for Helene.'

'And Helene is?' He raised his eyebrows.

'Well, she started out as a sort of *au pair* who helped me with the children, and then she just stayed on. Nowadays she helps me with everything from arranging the children's dental appointments to putting out the rubbish. Quite honestly, I don't know what I would do without her.'

He wanted to mention the fact that he knew she was a widow but somehow he couldn't quite bring himself to do so. He wasn't sure how recent her husband's death had been and he didn't want to cause her any unnecessary distress. On the other hand, if she assumed he didn't know, wouldn't she think it odd that he didn't mention the absence of a man in the house?

'The children have had their supper,' she said, as he deliberated over the problem, 'and they'll shortly be going to bed. 'I thought steak and a salad for us, if that's all right with you?'

'Wonderful,' he said, watching her as she began to uncork the wine. 'Here, let me do that.'

'OK.' As he took the bottle from her, his fingers briefly touched hers, and just for a moment he thought he detected a slight nervousness about her. He wondered if she did much entertaining. Almost as if she had read his thoughts, she said, 'You'll have to excuse me. I'm afraid I'm out of practice these days where entertaining is concerned…ever since my husband died…' She trailed off then, throwing a quick glance in his direction, she added, 'You know I'm a widow?'

'Yes,' he said, 'I do know, but only because Charlotte told Jamie and he told me.'

'You hadn't heard anything at St Benedict's?' There was curiosity in her voice now, almost as if she expected there to be gossip about her at work.

'No.' He frowned. 'Nothing at all. But why should I have heard anything?'

'Oh, no reason.' She shook her head dismissively. 'I just have to grill the steaks,' she said. 'How do you like yours?'

'Oh, rare to medium, please.' He paused, watching her as

she moved about the kitchen, appreciating the gracefulness of her movements. In an almost desperate attempt to quell a sudden and totally unexpected surge of desire, he said, 'So, did you do a lot of entertaining when your husband was alive?'

'Yes,' she said, 'all the time.'

'A bit like Claudia and Rory?'

'Well, perhaps not quite so much as them.' They both laughed then, growing serious again, she went on, 'My...my husband—Marcus—adored entertaining. In fact, I would go so far as to say that he actually liked entertaining more than being entertained.'

'Some people are like that.' He paused then reached a rapid decision and decided that while they were on the subject it was appropriate to establish a few more facts. 'How long is it since your husband died?'

'Two years,' she said. Watching her carefully as she spoke, Nathan saw a shadow cross her lovely features. 'He...he was killed. A car crash...a head-on collision.'

'I'm so sorry,' he said, and knew he meant it. 'It must have been dreadful for you.'

'Yes.' She swallowed and nodded. 'It was awful...'

'And for the children.'

'Yes. Worse for Charlotte than Lewis really. She was five, you see, and knew exactly what was going on. Lewis was only three and didn't really understand.' She gave a little shrug. 'Although he must have suffered a real sense of loss at his father not being around any more.'

'Were you working at St Benedict's at the time?' he asked, as he watched her remove the steaks from the grill and place them onto plates.

'I was working part time.' She placed the plates on the

table, which already bore a huge bowl of mixed salad and a basket of warmed bread rolls.

'And now you're working full time,' he observed as he took his place at the table.

'It's a case of having to,' she replied wryly as she, too, sat down and shook out her napkin. 'But having said that, I have to say I really enjoy my work and a lot of the reason for that is down to Helene. She is so good with the children and I find I don't have to worry about them when they are with her…so I suppose you could say that life is slowly getting back to normal.'

'But it will never be the same as it was,' he observed quietly. Only twenty-four hours ago he might have felt unable to make such an observation, but now, for some inexplicable reason, he knew he was able to do so, that it wouldn't be mis-construed.

'No,' she agreed, and he noticed that her hand shook slightly as she poured the wine. 'And I don't expect it to be. It can never be the same as it was…' Again that shadow that blurred her features and dimmed the light in her eyes. 'And as for entertaining,' she went on after a moment, a moment in which she composed herself again, 'well, I've never really got back into that again…'

'So I'm privileged tonight?' He raised his eyebrows.

'Yes, I suppose you could say that.' She laughed and he was relieved to see that she looked relaxed again. 'Do you do much entertaining?' she asked, almost as an afterthought.

'Lord, no,' he said. 'That sounds awful, doesn't it?' he added quickly when she raised her eyebrows. 'What I actually meant was that, like you—when I was with my wife, yes, we did use to entertain, not so much as you and your husband by the sound of it but, yes, we did have friends and family round for dinner and drinks and that sort of thing.' He shrugged. 'Like you say, it's different when you're on your own. I dare say I should make a bit more effort really because actually I do like cooking.' He paused. 'Perhaps you'd like me to cook for you one night?' As soon as he'd said it he wondered if he'd gone too far. It was one thing for Olivia to ask him round for supper after a day out with the children, it was another thing altogether for him to ask her back for a meal—in fact, it sounded suspiciously like a date. She didn't, however, seem fazed by the question. Instead, she smiled and nodded.

'That would be nice,' she said, then added a little anxiously, 'Is your steak all right?'

'It's delicious,' he replied.

They lingered over their meal for a long time, with Olivia producing a light dessert of fruit and ice cream followed by coffee, which she eventually suggested they take into the sun-room, whose doors were thrown open to embrace the coolness of the soft evening air. By this time the shadows were lengthening in the garden and the sun was sinking behind the western skyline of rooftops, aerials and chimneypots.

Oscar joined them, flopping down between them and panting heavily, his tongue hanging out. 'He knows it's nearly time for his evening walk,' said Olivia. 'It's Helene's turn this evening—she'll be home soon. We have to take it in turns so there's always someone here with the children.'

'It can't be easy,' he said, 'bringing up a family on your own.'

'No,' she agreed, 'it isn't.' They were silent for a moment then she threw him a sideways glance. 'How long is it since your divorce?' she asked.

'Nearly three years,' he replied. 'It's four years since we parted.'

'Do you think you will ever marry again?'

He drew in his breath sharply. No one had ever directly asked him that question before. 'I don't know,' he replied at last. 'I'm not at all sure that I could. When I married Susan, I imagined it would be for life. I trusted her utterly and completely and when she left me I was devastated. I'm not sure I could ever find it in me to have that sort of trust again.' He fell silent again, amazed at what he had just divulged to Olivia. He wasn't a man who expressed his feelings easily and here he was telling a comparative stranger his innermost thoughts and emotions.

'Do you know why she left you?' asked Olivia quietly. When he didn't immediately reply, she said, 'I'm sorry. Maybe this is too painful for you to talk about.'

'No,' he said, 'not at all. It all happened a long time ago and I should be over it by now.'

'But you're not,' she said, in the same quiet, almost gentle tone.

'No,' he admitted, 'I guess I'm not…completely.' He paused then took a deep breath. 'The reason Susan left me was because she'd met someone else. At the time I thought it was purely and simply that—she'd met someone right out of the blue and fallen in love with him. Now, with hindsight, I realise there must have been more to it than that. I realise there must have been something lacking in our relationship.'

'I'm not sure that is always the case…' Olivia began.

'Maybe not, but it was in our case. I'd not been investing enough time in our marriage. I was working incredibly long hours, leaving Susan and Jamie alone for longer and longer periods. I guess in the end she simply couldn't take it.'

'But that was your job, your career.' Olivia frowned. 'Surely she understood the nature of that?'

'Yes, I think she did, but that didn't necessarily mean she could cope with it. In the end she decided to return to work. That was where she met Martin—he was also married with children, but his marriage was already in trouble so I suppose you could say they were ready to fall into one another's arms.'

'It's still sad, though, especially when so many people get hurt—Jamie, and presumably Martin's children…and his wife.'

'You're right,' he said. Turning towards her as she refilled his coffee-cup, he said, 'But that's enough about me. What about you?'

'Me?' She looked faintly startled. 'What about me?'

'Do you think you will ever marry again, or is it still much too soon for you to say?' He noticed once again that her hand shook slightly as she set the coffee-pot down on the small wicker table between them.

'No,' she said. 'It's not too soon, because I already know the answer to that. I don't think I'll ever want to marry again.'

'I can understand that,' he said softly. 'You loved your husband and you don't think you would ever be able to love anyone like that again.' She didn't answer and he imagined she was too choked to speak. 'And when you've had such perfect trust, it would be very hard to think you could ever find trust like that again…'

'Actually,' she said, but that was as far as she got for at that moment there came the sound of a door shutting and Oscar lifted his head and gave a sound that was not quite a bark and not quite a yelp but somewhere in between. 'That will be Helene,' said Olivia. Oscar hauled himself up and padded out of the kitchen and she rose to her feet.

She looked troubled, Nathan thought, and he hoped that all this talk of their marriages and what had happened to each of them hadn't upset her too much. He had no time for further speculation, however, for at that moment a dark-haired woman had appeared in the doorway. She was talking as she came through the door, but on seeing Nathan she stopped dead. 'Oh,' she said. 'I sorry. I not know you have company.'

'It's all right, Helene,' said Olivia quickly. 'This is Mr Carrington—he's a colleague and a friend of the Lathwell-Foxes.' It didn't really explain what he was doing in her house late on a Sunday evening, after having had supper with her, and really, Nathan thought, she was under no obligation to explain her actions or her reasons to her employee. But the surprise on Helene's face registered the rarity of such occasions. 'Nathan.' She half turned towards him. 'This is Helene.'

'Hello, Helene.' He held out his hand. 'I'm very pleased to meet you,' he said. As the Frenchwoman briefly took his hand, he added, 'I've been hearing what a treasure you are.'

Helene laughed in embarrassment. 'I not a treasure,' she said. 'I do a job. I love my job. I love Olivia and the children… and, oh, yes, I love you, too.' She bent down and patted Oscar, who had positioned himself in front of her and was gazing up longingly into her face.

'He loves you, too,' said Olivia with a laugh, 'especially when you are about to take him for a walk.'

'Come on.' Helene laughed. 'I not forget.' Taking Oscar's lead from a hook behind the door, she disappeared down the passage again with a wave of her hand.

'You see what I mean?' said Olivia.

'I do indeed,' he agreed. He paused. 'It's time I was going,' he said. 'It's been a lovely evening, Olivia. I've enjoyed it very much—thank you.'

'I've enjoyed it, too,' she said.

'Like I said, you must let me cook for you some time.'

'I'd like that,' she said.

She led the way through the house to the front door, where she paused for a moment with one hand on the catch and turned towards him as if she was uncertain quite what should happen next. He caught the scent of her perfume, a heady, musky fragrance so completely in keeping with that exotic aura about her that he had noticed at their very first meeting. As he stood looking down at her and her eyes met his, it seemed that all the events of that extraordinary day seemed to reach a peak and culminated in a moment of totally unexpected magic between them.

It was without the slightest hesitation that he bent his head and it seemed the most natural thing in the world for his lips to meet hers in a kiss that somehow seemed to make time stand still. Her mouth beneath his felt soft, tasted sweet, and even as he felt an uncontrollable leap of desire that sent his senses spinning into oblivion, it was over and she was drawing away.

He stared at her in consternation. What in the world had he done? Had he totally misread the situation? 'I'm...I'm sorry...' he said. 'That shouldn't have happened.'

'Really?' she said lightly, arching her eyebrows. 'I can't think why not. It was a rather lovely end to a perfect day.' And while still he floundered for something else to say and at the same time desperately tried to control the clamouring of his body, she lifted her hand and very gently touched the side of his face. 'Goodnight, Nathan,' she said.

Seconds later he was in his car, wondering if he'd dreamt the whole thing, wondering if all that had happened had simply been a figment of his imagination.

CHAPTER SIX

'I WANT you to try some different medication. I have to warn you there won't be any overnight miracles but I do hope that when I see Jonty again in three months' time there will have been at least some improvement.'

'I do hope so, Dr Gilbert.' Jonty Miles's mother Dee looked totally exhausted. She was in her mid-thirties but looked ten years older as the constant strain of caring for her thirteen-year-old autistic son took its toll. There were dark circles around her eyes from constantly disturbed nights, as Jonty demanded attention every couple of hours, while her features looked pinched and drawn and her hair lank and lifeless.

'Have you been able to arrange any respite care?' asked Olivia as she handed the prescription to Dee, only for Jonty to try to snatch it out of her hand. When he failed to do so he began shouting and banging the desk in front of him.

'His care manager is looking into it.' Dee raised her voice over Jonty's shouting. 'But my husband is reluctant for him to go.'

'Why is that?' Olivia frowned. Usually in these cases the reverse was true as carers became desperate for respite care.

'He says that by the time Jonty comes back to us his routine will have been so disrupted and it would take him so long to settle down that it isn't worth him going in the first place.'

'I'm sorry to hear that,' said Olivia, 'but even if that is the case, I still think you and your husband and your other son need some time to recharge your batteries.'

'Well, we'll have to see.' Dee stood up. 'Come on, Jonty,' she said, 'we're going home now.' Immediately the boy's demeanour changed. He stopped banging the desk and fell silent. 'Goodbye, Dr Gilbert,' said Dee, taking Jonty's hand.

'Goodbye, Dee. Goodbye, Jonty.' Olivia sighed as she watched them leave her consulting room. Sometimes she felt she had very little to offer those of her patients with such long-term, ongoing conditions as Jonty's, but at the same time she also felt that the parents seemed to derive some small measure of comfort in their uphill struggle by these routine visits to the paediatric outpatient clinic, even if it was only for a chat. And if that was the case, it was well worthwhile.

Already that morning, apart from Jonty, she'd seen a child with cerebral palsy, another with spina bifida, one with sickle cell anaemia and two with attention deficit hyperactivity disorder. Jonty had been the last child on that morning's list and after she'd typed up the notes and saved them on her computer, Olivia left her consulting room and made her way onto the paediatric ward.

Kirstin was in charge of the ward that morning, and instinctively Olivia knew that as soon as she saw her Kirstin would want to discuss the events of the weekend.

Olivia hadn't yet seen Nathan since arriving at St Benedict's that day, but strangely she gradually became aware that, albeit unconsciously, she was looking for him. Even on her arrival in the staff car park she'd found herself casually looking around for his car, momentarily thinking that he hadn't yet arrived then, on catching sight of it tucked away in a far corner, experiencing a sudden stab of…well, of excitement really.

Later, *en route* to the paediatric clinic, on passing the cardiac department, she'd caught a snatch of conversation between two men and had recognised Nathan's voice. He'd been out of her sight but she'd almost found herself going back, showing herself, seeking him out, anything, just to pass the time of day with him. Which really, when she considered it, was completely ridiculous. She liked Nathan, of course she did. He was a pleasant and friendly man and she'd very much enjoyed the time spent in his company the previous day—the time at the fun day with the children and, later, the supper they'd shared and the conversation they'd enjoyed. Even that kiss, which had taken her completely by surprise but which she'd actually enjoyed, partly because it had been such a long time since anyone had kissed her, partly because it had seemed so natural and partly because, she also was forced to admit, Nathan was a very attractive man. But no matter how she felt, it couldn't lead to anything more.

The moment Kirstin caught sight of Olivia she launched straight in to an in-depth analysis of the fun day and the events surrounding it. 'It was brilliant, wasn't it?' she demanded. When Olivia agreed she went on, 'It raised over a thousand pounds for the ward and the children all had such fun. And as for that treasure hunt, well, it was a stroke of genius. Rory was brilliant with the children and so was Nathan—don't you agree?'

'Er…yes…yes, I suppose so,' Olivia said, without looking up from the records she was desperately trying to concentrate on.

'I told you he was divorced, didn't I?' Kirstin, it seemed, was far from letting the matter drop.

'Yes, you did,' Olivia agreed.

'Does his son live with him, do you know?'

'No, he lives with his mother and her new partner in Chester.'

'Really?' Olivia was aware that Kirstin had turned to look at her but she scrupulously avoided eye contact.

'So does that mean he doesn't get to see the boy very much—Jamie, isn't it?'

'Yes, that's right, and I rather gathered that he sees him as much as he can. I think it was a bit easier when Nathan lived in Oxford but it's that bit further now he's here in London.' She paused then, glancing around the ward, she said, 'I think I'll just go and have a chat with Sara—it looks like her op has been cleared for tomorrow.'

'Hang on a minute,' said Kirstin. 'How do you know all this?'

'All what?' Olivia looked up in feigned innocence.

'All this about Nathan Carrington's domestic arrangements.'

'He told me.' Olivia shrugged.

'But you didn't even know he was divorced until I told you during the barbeque, then they had the treasure hunt and soon after that he was gone—not a lot of time for cosy, in-depth discussions...'

'We talked later...' Olivia knew she was beaten and would have to come clean with Kirstin, who seemed to have the knack of extracting information out of her.

'What do you mean, later...?' Kirstin's eyes narrowed.

Olivia sighed. 'When we got home Lewis found he had Jamie's sunglasses in his pocket so I phoned Nathan to see if Jamie was still with him.'

'And was he?' Kirstin's interest was definitely aroused now.

'No, his mother had already collected him.'

'So…what did you do?'

She took a deep breath. 'I asked him if he'd like to come over for a bit of supper.' She spoke in a brisk, matter-of-fact fashion but Kirstin was not to be fobbed off by that.

'Hah!' she said. 'Now we're getting somewhere.'

'Kirstin.' Olivia tried to sound patient. 'I don't know what you mean. There's absolutely nothing going on so I don't want you to go reading anything in to it.'

'But Nathan Carrington did come and have supper with you—right?'

'Yes, right, but like I say—'

'Yes, yes, I know—but it's a start. Let's face it, Olivia, you've been shut away on your own for far too long. It's high time you had some fun in your life again.'

'So you keep telling me,' said Olivia dryly.

'Well it's true,' Kirstin protested. 'Like I've said before, Marcus would never have wanted this…'

'None of us know what Marcus would or wouldn't have wanted,' said Olivia. She spoke more sharply than she had intended and she couldn't fail to notice Kirstin's quick glance of surprise. 'What I mean is,' she went on hurriedly, 'what I now do or don't do can't have any bearing on what Marcus would have wished.'

'Well, no, I realise that,' said Kirstin, 'but it seemed to me that you were thinking in some way that it would be disloyal to Marcus to embark on another relationship when in actual fact research has shown that it is those who were in the happiest marriages who are the most anxious to enter into a new relationship if something happens to their partner…and knowing how sublimely happy you and Marcus were, I just thought…'

'I know what you thought,' said Olivia, 'but, contrary to

your research, I can assure you I'm in absolutely no hurry to go dashing into any sort of relationship.'

As she spoke she wondered what Kirstin would say if she knew the truth, but then she dismissed the thought. No one knew that and if she had anything to do with it no one ever would, even if in a moment of madness last night she'd come within a whisker of telling Nathan. Only Helene's return had stopped her from doing so, and now in the cold light of day she was relieved for that intervention.

'But you enjoyed your supper with Nathan?'

'Oh, yes,' Olivia said. 'He's very good company, and I have to say it's rather nice to have a no-strings-attached friendship with a member of the opposite sex.'

'Platonic, you mean?' Kirstin raised one eyebrow.

'Well, yes, I suppose you could call it that.'

'My mother always used to say there's no such thing,' said Kirstin with a sniff. After a pause she said, 'So, does he know that?'

'Does who know what?' Olivia looked deliberately vague, knowing full well what Kirstin meant.

'Him—Nathan Carrington—does he know this relationship is to be purely platonic?'

'What relationship? Honestly, Kirstin, you really are the limit. One supper doesn't constitute a relationship.'

'So was that all there was to it? Are you telling me he didn't suggest anything else?'

'Well…'

'Yes, go on…'

'He did say something about cooking supper for me one night.'

'So we're talking relationship.'

'Hardly!' said Olivia with a laugh. 'And even if we are—
which we aren't, I'm just as certain that he would also only
be interested in a friendship—I got the impression he's still
suffering from the fallout from his divorce. I can't imagine
he'll be too eager to leap into anything else.'

'Well…we shall see,' said Kirstin darkly. The phone on her
desk rang and she lifted the receiver to answer it.

Seeing her chance to escape from her friend's well-
meaning but relentless questioning, Olivia left the office and
made her way down the ward to where Sara was deeply engaged in colouring a picture with her mother Sharon.

'Hello, Sara.' Olivia stopped in front of the table and was
rewarded with a heart-stopping smile from the young girl
who then, with the tip of her tongue protruding from the
corner of her mouth, returned to her colouring with fierce con-
centration. 'So, Sharon,' said Olivia, 'it looks like this time
it's really going to happen.'

'I can hardly believe it,' said Sharon, 'after all this time.'
She looked up at Olivia as she spoke and Olivia noticed the
trace of tears on her face.

'Why don't we go over there and have a coffee?' she said,
nodding towards the visitor area where a coffee-pot bubbled
invitingly. Without a word Sharon stood up and Olivia indicated to one of the carers to keep an eye on Sara.

Moments later the two of them were settled in easy chairs
beside a low table with a cup of coffee apiece. 'It's under-
standable that you will be anxious,' said Olivia, opening the
conversation, 'but you can rest assured that Sara will receive
the very best of expertise and care.'

'Oh, I know that.' Nervously Sharon began shredding a
paper tissue. 'But…' She trailed off uncertainly.

'Something has upset you, hasn't it?' Olivia lowered her head in order to be able to look into Sharon's face.

'Yes,' Sharon admitted, 'it has.'

'Want to tell me about it?'

'It was on Friday when I went to collect my son from school. One of the other mothers asked about Sara and I said that hopefully she would be having her operation this week. Later I overheard another mother say it was a waste of time and money operating on someone like Sara—that she probably wouldn't live long anyway and that it would be far better to use the money on someone who would really benefit.' She took a huge breath. 'It really upset me, Dr Gilbert, I don't mind telling you.'

'I'm sure it did, Sharon,' said Olivia quietly, 'but I really think you must try and put it out of your mind. It was a thoughtless remark…'

'But do you think that's how most people see it?'

'No, of course I don't. Any right-thinking person would agree that Sara is entitled to the same treatment as any other child. And as for her not living long—well, there was a time once when life expectancy for Down's syndrome sufferers was much less than it is today. Nowadays, those with the condition can live quite happy and fulfilled lives, sometimes into their sixties. Forget that remark, Sharon, put it down to ignorance. Sara is precious. Every life is precious—never forget that.'

'Thank you, Dr Gilbert. Honestly, you are all so kind. Mr Carrington came in to see Sara this morning and he said everything is ready for tomorrow. And as for Sister Chandler, well, she treats Sara just like she was one of her own children.'

'So, no more worries, then?' asked Olivia as she drained her coffee-cup.

'Sara won't know anything, will she?'

'No, she won't. She'll be given a pre-med, which will sedate her, then she'll be given a general anaesthetic, after which she won't know another thing until she wakes up.'

'Will she come straight back here?' asked Sharon, looking around the ward.

'No, she'll go into a high-dependency unit for a few days, where she'll receive one-to-one nursing, then she will come back here.'

'What about pain? I'm worried there will be a lot of pain and she won't understand why. I don't think she has any concept of what an operation is or what it will involve.'

'No,' Olivia agreed, 'I don't suppose she does, but you can rest assured that her pain levels will be very carefully monitored and controlled. I think you will find that she will cope with the whole situation much better than you think.'

'Oh, I hope so, Dr Gilbert. I do hope so.'

'Now, do you have anything else you want to ask me?' said Olivia.

'Just one thing, Doctor. Will you be in Theatre?'

'Yes, I will.' Olivia nodded. 'Sara has been my patient for a long time and I want to be there for this to keep a close eye on the proceedings.' Her reply seemed to satisfy Sharon then as an afterthought Olivia went on, 'Do you have anyone who will sit with you during the operation?'

'Yes,' Sharon replied. 'My sister will be here with me, and Sara's grandmother—that's my ex-husband's mother. She's devoted to Sara.'

'That's good.' Olivia smiled. 'Family support is essential at a time like this.'

She left the children's ward shortly after that, intending to return to her consulting room, but just before she reached the door, at the end of the corridor she caught sight of Nathan and in spite of her earlier protestations to Kirstin that her feelings towards him were purely platonic, to her consternation she felt her heart leap.

He waited for her, watching her walk towards him. 'Hi,' he said softly, and as her heart settled down it began to melt.

'Hello,' she said, then couldn't think of another single thing to say.

'I just wanted to say thank you,' he said, coming to her rescue, 'for last night. It was lovely.'

'Oh, it was nothing,' she said, trying to dismiss it.

'Well, I enjoyed it,' he said firmly.

'Oh,' she said, not wanting him to misunderstand, 'so did I.'

'I'm glad to hear that,' he said, 'because if that's the case, you won't mind repeating the exercise.'

'Of course not,' she said, she hoped lightly, in a matter-of-fact, platonic sort of way. 'You said you would cook next time—I shall hold you to that.'

'I'll arrange something,' he said. 'Maybe next weekend?'

'That would be nice,' she murmured. He looked impossibly handsome and very masculine in his green scrubs, straight from Theatre. His dark hair, lightly gelled, looked wet while those green eyes seemed to be able to see into her very soul and somehow seemed to throw her off key. 'I've…I've just been talking to Sharon,' she said, looking away quickly, suddenly desperate for something to say.

'Sharon?' He looked faintly puzzled but at the same time almost irritated, as if he didn't want the conversation diverted away from themselves and the almost intimate, personal moment they had just shared.

'Yes, Sharon Middleton.'

'Oh, Sara's mum.' With obvious reluctance he drew his focus back to work-related topics and away from themselves.

'Yes, we talked through the procedures for tomorrow,' she replied.

'And is she happy?'

'Well, she's very happy that it's going to happen at last but she'd been upset by a thoughtless remark she'd overheard.' She went on to tell Nathan what had happened.

'People can be so cruel,' he said when she had finished.

'I hope I managed to reassure her,' she said.

'I'm sure you did—you seem to have a knack for that sort of thing.'

'Now, how can you possibly know something like that on such short acquaintance?' Somehow she'd regained her composure and she raised her eyebrows as she posed the question.

'Ah,' he said, 'I just know these things—put it down to instinct if you like. You ladies don't have the monopoly on intuition you know.'

'I wouldn't for one moment lay claim to that,' she retorted lightly, then, changing the subject, she said, 'Did you tell Jamie about his sunglasses?'

'I did,' he replied. 'I called him early this morning and told him.'

'No doubt he was pleased he hadn't lost them,' she said.

'Yes, I guess he was, but do you know, he seemed far more pleased and interested in the fact that I'd been to your house for supper.'

'Really?' She'd been about to move away to go into her consulting room but she paused, intrigued by what he was saying.

'Yes, he wanted to know all about it. Where your house

was, what it was like, whether or not I saw Charlotte and Lewis. Oh, and Oscar. He wanted to know all about Oscar.'

'But how did he know about Oscar—in the first place, I mean?'

'I think Lewis had told him—they'd been discussing pets apparently.'

'They all seem to have covered a tremendous amount of ground in the short time they were together,' said Olivia with a laugh.

'They did indeed,' Nathan agreed. 'But I guess that's kids for you—they don't pull any punches, do they? He also wanted to know when he could come down again.'

'So what did you say to that?'

'I said I would be happy for him to come whenever, but that really it was up to his mother.'

'Is she co-operative over things like that?'

'Mostly, but she can be a bit awkward on occasion. Anyway, we'll have to see what we can work out.'

'Charlotte and Lewis will be pleased, they haven't stopped talking about Jamie and how cool he was. Anyway, Nathan...' she glanced at her watch '...I must go. I have another clinic shortly.'

'OK.' Briefly his eyes met hers. 'If I don't see you before then, I'll see you in Theatre tomorrow morning. You will be there, won't you?'

'Absolutely.' Unflinchingly she returned his gaze then, suddenly overwhelmed by something in his eyes, something she was at a loss to define, she turned away quickly.

'Great day, Sunday, Rory—Jamie thought so, too.'

'Glad you enjoyed it,' said Rory. 'We did as well.' It was

later that same day. Nathan had just finished in Theatre and had met Rory coming out of the adjoining theatre suite.

'Claudia was saying she thought you and a certain paediatrician seemed to be getting on rather well,' Rory went on as they fell into step.

'Claudia is an eternal matchmaker,' said Nathan, 'and come to that, I rather suspect that you may be as well.'

'Don't know what you're talking about.' Rory shook his head, his expression deliberately vague then, with a little chuckle, he went on, 'But even if we are, is there anything so wrong in that? Olivia's a gorgeous young woman—you can't deny that.'

'I wouldn't dream of denying it,' Nathan replied.

'Well, there you are, then. I don't know what you're waiting for—there you are, young, free and not that bad-looking, I suppose…'

'Thanks for that,' Nathan replied dryly.

'Don't mention it.' Rory grinned. 'So, like I say…what's stopping you?'

'Who says I'm looking for that sort of relationship?' Nathan raised one eyebrow.

'Well, if you're not, it's high time you were,' Rory replied. 'You've got to put the past behind you, Nathan, and get on with your life. OK, what happened with Susan was all very upsetting but I really don't think you should let that interfere with your future.'

'Maybe I'm happy as I am,' said Nathan mildly.

'Maybe you are.' Rory looked a little taken aback. 'But, actually, I don't think you are—and neither does Claudia, if you must know. She thinks it's high time you found yourself a suitable woman and settled down again.'

'Does she, now? And she thinks Olivia Gilbert is suitable material for me, does she?'

'Actually, yes, she does.' Any irony seemed lost on Rory. 'It's two years now since Olivia's husband died—I dare say she's thinking it's time she moved on. I know she has her children but, then, you have Jamie…'

'So what was he like?'

'What was who like?' Rory frowned as if he'd completely lost the thread of the conversation.

'Olivia's late husband.'

'Marcus?' Rory paused, considering. 'Well, Marcus was Marcus. High-flying. A successful barrister. Mind like a razor.'

'Did you like him?' asked Nathan.

'Yes…he was OK, I guess… Claudia adored him but I suppose he had that effect on most women, if I'm honest. There was something about him, though…'

'Yes?' said Nathan.

'Well, it was probably nothing really, but in all the years I knew him I never really felt I did know him, if you know what I mean.'

'Yes, I think I get your drift.'

'I always felt there was another side to him, a side he kept well hidden from the rest of us.'

'Was he a good father?' Suddenly Nathan felt a bit uneasy talking about Olivia's family in this way but, he had to admit, there was a part of him that was intensely curious.

'Oh, yes.' Rory nodded. 'He adored his kids and they him. And Olivia, well, I guess she worshipped the ground he walked on.'

'So what actually happened—the accident I mean? Olivia said a head-on crash.'

'Yes, that's right—with a truck apparently. He was dead on arrival when they got him to hospital. Terrible blow to Olivia and his family and a great loss to the legal profession.'

At that moment someone called Rory from one of the treatment rooms and with a wave of his hand he was gone, leaving Nathan to continue on alone to his consulting room.

Olivia intrigued him—there were no two ways about it. If he was strictly honest, she'd done so right from the start, from the very moment he'd caught that seductive glimpse of her in Rory and Claudia's garden, and she'd continued to do so ever since. And now, if anything, since finding out more about her—like the fact that she was a widow and was bringing up two children on her own—she intrigued him even more. He'd enjoyed the evening he'd spent at her home, almost more than he cared to admit—even to himself—and there was no denying that everything about her he found attractive, from the way she dressed and moved, to her gracious and elegant home and the way she lived her life.

The kiss they had shared had stirred his emotions to such an extent that he hadn't been able to get her out of his mind, and the previous night she'd haunted his dreams so much that on arriving at St Benedict's that morning he'd found himself looking for her everywhere, straining his ears for the sound of her voice. But he'd had to wait until nearly midday when, after a particularly gruelling morning in Theatre, where he'd carried out a triple bypass operation, he'd caught sight of her in the corridor as he'd been about to enter his consulting room.

He'd waited for her, and she'd seemed pleased to see him. They'd chatted briefly about the night before, about the Middleton family, the children, even her dog—anything really to keep her talking for a little longer. But in the end she'd had to go, said she had another clinic to take, but at least there had been further mention of him cooking a meal for her next time and she'd seemed quite keen on the idea.

He was even beginning to wonder whether he wasn't ready after all to start another relationship in spite of his previous misgivings. If he was, Olivia was definitely the sort of woman he would choose.

He was decidedly restless again that evening, and as before he found himself wishing he could find a reason to phone her. The night before, when he had felt that way, she had totally surprised him by phoning him, but somehow he didn't think that would happen again, and if he phoned her on some pretext, maybe it would give her the wrong impression, allowing her to think that he was hounding her when she had made it plain that she wasn't really interesting in starting another relationship. But had she meant it? She'd told him that before that kiss they'd shared—maybe now she felt differently. But he mustn't go reading too much into that one kiss, he told himself firmly. After all, it may have meant no more to Olivia than a simple way of saying goodnight.

But it had been more than that, hadn't it? He was sure it had. So, if she didn't want any sort of long-term relationship, maybe a short fling would be the answer? But even as the thought entered his head he dismissed it. Somehow he doubted that Olivia was the type of woman who would go in for a short fling, and if he was really honest, that wouldn't be what he would want either. He'd had a couple of those since Susan and they'd left him feeling strange, cut adrift somehow and only briefly satisfied. He couldn't imagine something like that with Olivia, feared they would simply end up hurting

one another, and that was something he couldn't even bear the
thought of. Rory had been quite brutal really, telling him in a
roundabout way that it was high time he pulled himself together and got on with his life. Well, maybe it was. But he
wasn't at all sure that Olivia would be the one who would help
him to do so, even though the very thought of that filled him
with a desperate sort of longing.

In the end, in a final attempt to curb his restlessness, he
decided to ring Jamie.

Susan answered on the tenth ring. She sounded snappy and
impatient and Nathan was thankful for the distance that separated them. He remembered Susan's moods only too well.
'Is Jamie around?' he asked, after saying hello.

'Again?' She sounded incredulous. 'You spent the whole
weekend with him, and you only spoke to him this morning.'

'I didn't realise our time was rationed,' he said, carefully
not allowing impatience to creep into his own voice while at
the same time feeling that sense of exasperation that Susan
always seemed to arouse in him.

'It's not,' she retorted. 'Of course it's not. I'll fetch him for
you.' She must have pressed the silent button on her phone
because he didn't hear another sound until Jamie answered.

'Hello—Dad?' he said, and even he sounded surprised. 'Is
anything wrong?'

'No,' Nathan replied. 'I just fancied a chat with you, that's
all. But, hey, listen, if this is a bad time, I could call back.'

'No, it's OK,' said Jamie, but there still seemed to be a wary
note in his voice.

'You weren't eating or anything?'

'No, we've had supper.'

'Oh, that's all right, then—it was just that your mother

sounded a bit…' He hesitated, uncertain what adjective he could use to best describe Susan's mood. 'A bit fraught.'

'Yes,' Jamie replied, 'she is. Her and Martin have had a huge row.'

'Jamie I'm not sure you should be telling me this—' Nathan began, but Jamie interrupted him.

'It's OK,' he said misunderstanding the reason for Nathan's caution. 'They can't hear me. Martin's gone out and Mum is upstairs. She said she was going to have a long soak in the bath.'

'So this row, did it involve you in any way?'

'Not really,' Jamie replied. 'It happens all the time,' he added. 'I'm sort of used to it now but…I still wish I could come and live with you, Dad.'

Nathan took a deep breath. He hadn't realised there was so much friction between Susan and her partner. 'I wish you could as well,' he said carefully, 'but it was all agreed when your mother and I parted that you would stay with her.'

'Yeah, I know, but I do miss you, Dad.'

'Yes, I know you do.' As Nathan replied he felt the beginning of a huge lump forming in his throat. 'And I miss you as well.' He took a deep breath. 'Maybe,' he said, 'we need to find ways of you coming here a little more often and perhaps for longer periods—would you like that?' Even as he spoke he knew that such a plan would be difficult, especially where his work was concerned. But, hell, those difficulties could be overcome—plenty of other people he knew had to juggle the demands of family and a high-powered job. Maybe what he needed was someone like Helene. He smiled at the thought.

'That would be cool,' said Jamie.

'Well, we'll have to see what we can do…'

'Did you see Mrs Gilbert today?' Jamie asked, after a longish pause.

'Yes, I did—only briefly, though, because she was taking her children's clinics and I was in Theatre. But I shall see her tomorrow because we will both be in Theatre as we are both involved with the same patient.'

'I like Mrs Gilbert,' said Jamie.

'Yes, Jamie, so do I. She's a really nice lady. Now, tell me, how was school today?'

'Boring,' said Jamie.

'In what way boring?'

'We had history—the Wars of the Roses. I can't see any point in doing all that when I'm going to be a surgeon.'

Nathan was still chuckling some little while later when he hung up. It always did him good to talk to Jamie. This time, however, alongside feeling good, he also found himself anxious about Jamie's revelations on the state of his mother's relationship with her partner. But in spite of that, he couldn't help but be pleased that Jamie had seemed so happy with the time he'd spent with the Gilbert family.

CHAPTER SEVEN

NATHAN glanced around the theatre at his assembled team: his assistant, Dr Aziz; Olivia, and Diana. There was also the theatre staff—Sister Gawn, the scrub nurse and three operating department assistants. Two students were to observe, too. 'Good morning, everyone,' he said. 'Are we all here?'

There were murmurings and nods of assent and Nathan began his pre-op briefing. 'This little lady…' he nodded towards the anaesthetised patient, who was being wheeled into the theatre by an orderly '…is Sara Middleton, who is twelve years old. She was born with atrio-ventricular defects—namely a largish hole in the middle of her heart between the atria and the ventricles. It is our task this morning to close this hole by means of a patch. Dr Gilbert.' His gaze found Olivia and lingered there, observing the slender figure in its theatre greens. A stray tendril of dark hair had escaped onto the vulnerable nape of her neck and when she half turned towards him, above the edge of her mask, he saw those lustrous dark eyes. 'Would you like to fill us in on other details relevant to this case, please?'

'Of course,' she murmured, then, mainly for the benefit of the students, she said, 'Sara was born with Down's syndrome.

She also has a gastro-intestinal condition, for which she receives drug therapy, and asthma, which is well controlled with corticosteroid inhalers. Ideally, it would have been preferable to have carried out this procedure when Sara was younger but she was never considered strong enough to withstand it.'

'And now?' It was one of the students who posed the crucial question.

'It has to be carried out now,' Olivia replied. 'Sara's breathing is becoming increasingly laboured of late and there is too much strain being placed on her heart and her lungs.'

'What about her asthma?' asked the second student.

Diana answered. 'I included salbutamol with the aminophylline and pethedine pre-med to dilate her airways, and I've also included hydrocortisone with the anaesthetic.' While Diana was explaining the precautions she'd taken with Sara's medication, the theatre staff were preparing Sara, covering her with green drapes then applying iodine to her chest area and linking her up to a heart monitor and the other mass of equipment that was essential to maintain her stability throughout the operation. One of the ODAs moved the diathermy machine into place, ready to control bleeding, and another switched on Nathan's favoured music. As the strains of 'Summer' from Vivaldi's *Four Seasons* filled the theatre, he stepped forward and prepared to make his incision.

Olivia stretched and rubbed her neck and shoulders, pulling off her cap and mask before disposing of them in the waste bin. It had been an intense and sometimes gruelling few hours as Nathan had attempted to give Sara a better quality of life, and now it was over. All that remained was for Nathan and herself to go and talk to Sharon. She waited for him as he disposed of his own cap, mask and plastic apron, her eyes meeting his as he joined her. He looked tired and weary after the long battle and her heart went out to him.

'Come on,' he said. 'We'll go and see Sharon together, shall we?'

'Yes,' Olivia said, and together, in silence, they walked out of the theatre unit and down the corridor to the relatives' room.

Sharon was standing in front of the window, gazing out at the London traffic that roared up and down far below, while her sister and Sara's grandmother drank coffee and with unseeing eyes flicked through magazines. As Nathan and Olivia entered the room, Sharon swung round and the other two looked up sharply.

'How is she?' Predictably it was Sharon who posed the question. Her gaze raked Nathan's face for some sign or clue as to what had happened.

He took a deep breath. 'It was a far more complicated and difficult procedure than I had envisaged,' he said.

'But she is all right?' Desperation filled Sharon's eyes.

'She's very poorly, Sharon.' It was Olivia who, recognising a mother's anguished need, answered her question.

'But she's alive?' whispered Sharon.

'Yes, she's alive,' Nathan replied. 'She's in Recovery at the moment, but I have to warn you she is in a very weakened state.'

'But she is going to be all right, isn't she?' Sara's grandmother posed the crucial question.

'Well, we hope so,' said Nathan. 'But as I explained to you, the whole procedure was much more involved than we had expected. At one point during the operation it was necessary to resuscitate Sara.'

'Oh, dear God…' whispered the older woman.

'Can I see her?' A determined light entered Sharon's eyes and she drew herself up.

'When she comes out of Recovery she'll be moved to the intensive-care wing of the children's unit,' said Olivia. 'You'll be able to see her then, Sharon. And, rest assured, she will receive the highest quality of care that is possible while she is there. Now, if you'd like to wait here for just a little longer, someone will come and tell you when you can go and see her.'

'That wasn't the news I'd wanted to give them,' said Nathan tightly as he and Olivia left the relatives' room.

'I know,' said Olivia quietly, 'but there's still a chance she will pull through, Nathan.'

'A slender one,' he said grimly. 'It really was far more involved and complicated than I had imagined.'

'You have done everything you possibly could,' Olivia tried to reassure him, but he still seemed tormented by the false assumption that he could somehow have done more.

'I could do with a drink,' he said.

'Then why don't we go down to the social club and have one?' said Olivia.

'I make it a rule never to drink after operating,' he said, 'especially when I think I'm in need of one.'

'In that case,' she said calmly, 'it had better be coffee in the canteen…' She paused and threw him a sidelong glance. His profile was set and his brows drawn together. 'Or does caffeine come in the same category as alcohol?'

'No.' His face cleared and he managed a brief smile. 'Coffee will be fine. You will join me?' he added, almost anxiously, she thought.

'Of course I will,' she replied, recognising the extreme postop tension he was going through. 'And then we'll go up to ITU together and see Sara when she gets back from Recovery.'

'Thanks,' he said briefly.

'Don't mention it. I need to know she's all right as much as you do—I've known Sara a long time.'

Ten minutes later they were seated at a quiet corner table in the staff canteen, a large coffee-pot between them together with a couple of small packets of chocolate digestive biscuits. 'I thought we needed to boost our sugar levels,' he'd said ruefully, as he'd placed the biscuits on the table.

'You could be right,' she said with a smile.

'You must think I'm mad, not having a drink,' he said after a while, throwing her a wary glance as she poured the coffee.

'Not at all…' She shrugged.

'I don't have a problem with alcohol but I had a friend once—a fellow surgeon,' he said slowly. 'I would never have described him as a drinker, he just enjoyed an occasional drink socially, but as time went on he got into the habit of having a drink after each time he operated. In the end he couldn't handle it…'

'What happened to him?' asked Olivia.

'He had to leave the profession,' Nathan replied. 'The last I heard he was drying out in some clinic. I vowed then I wouldn't be tempted down the same road.'

'Very wise,' said Olivia. She reflected silently for a moment. 'I don't think,' she went on, 'the public realise the strain we sometimes work under and the tremendous responsibilities we bear.'

'That's true.' He gave a little shrug. 'But I guess it goes with the territory.' They were silent for a while then suddenly he looked up from his coffee, which he'd been stirring almost absent-mindedly, and as if reaching a sudden decision he said, 'I spoke to Jamie again last night.'

'Really?' She raised her eyebrows then, when he remained silent, she said, 'Was he all right?'

'I'm not sure really.'

'Oh?' She paused, watching him intently, aware of the shadow that had crossed his face at mention of his son. 'Want to talk about it?' she went on after a moment.

'He…he said he wants to come and live with me,' he said at last.

'Oh,' she said, adding carefully, 'Would that be at all possible?'

He drew in his breath sharply. 'I really don't know. From a purely practical point of view, I'm not at all sure how I would work things out but…well, you manage, don't you?'

'Yes, I do,' she said slowly, 'but I have to say that's largely down to Helene—I'm not sure how I would manage without her.'

'I guess I would also need someone like Helene,' he said ruefully.

'So how did you leave things with Jamie?'

'Well, I suggested that perhaps we could find ways of him spending more time with me, but I didn't exactly go so far as to discuss the possibility of him living with me.'

'What about his mother—what would her reaction be to this?'

'I don't know.' He shook his head and for a moment looked weary and sad. Once again Olivia felt a sudden rush of emotion towards him. 'When we parted,' he continued after a moment, 'it was agreed that Jamie would stay with his mother because that really did seem the more practical option.'

'So what do you think has brought this about—Jamie wanting to come to you?'

'Two things really, I think,' he said slowly. 'The fact that I've now moved further away and I think Jamie is concerned that would inevitably mean we'll see much less of each other…'

'And the other?' she said.

'Sorry?' He looked up.

'You said two things,' she prompted.

'Oh, yes.' He hesitated. 'Well, it came out last night that Susan and her partner Martin argue all the time. I didn't know that before. Jamie's never said…'

'But he did last night?'

'Yes, apparently they had a huge row last night just before I phoned. Susan answered and seemed very fraught—I happened to mention as much to Jamie and that's when he told me.'

'Oh, dear,' said Olivia. 'That must be so hard for you.'

'Well, it's Jamie I worry about… Anyway, that's quite enough of my problems…I shouldn't be bothering you with them…'

'Not at all,' she said quickly. 'I'm only too glad to be of any help—even if it's only listening.'

'Thanks,' he said, and his eyes met hers. 'It does help to talk. I've never really talked to anyone before about Jamie or about Susan and my divorce, come to that…'

'Maybe it's time you did,' she said. 'I'm always happy to lend an ear if it helps.' Even as she said it she knew she meant it—she was prepared to help him if she could. She liked him, maybe more than that. She didn't really know but the spontaneity of their closeness had certainly taken her unawares. And she'd liked Jamie and it troubled her to think that either of them might be upset or unhappy in any way.

They finished their coffee then made their way to the high-dependency wing of the paediatric unit where they found that Sara had been brought in from Recovery and that her mother was seated beside her bed, which was surrounded by the monitors and technological equipment necessary for Sara's recuperation.

Sharon, who was holding Sara's hand, looked up as Olivia and Nathan approached, and Olivia noticed the tell-tale sign of tears on her cheeks. Nathan leaned over the bed and gently, almost tenderly smoothed Sara's hair back from her forehead. 'She's a little fighter,' he said. 'I'll give her that.'

'Oh, she is, that,' whispered Sharon. 'All we need now is a miracle so that she'll pull through.'

While Nathan had a word with the duty doctor and the sister-in-charge, Olivia sat beside Sharon as she maintained her vigil over her daughter.

'Have your family seen Sara?' she asked after a while.

'Yes, just briefly,' Sharon replied, 'but Sister said we couldn't all stay. I wanted them to go home but they won't budge—they've gone back to the relatives' room.'

'I'm so glad you've got some good support,' said Olivia, squeezing her arm.

A little later she and Nathan left the unit and it went unspoken between them that neither of them expected Sara to make it through the night.

The following morning when she woke up, Olivia's first thought was of Sara, then she thought of Nathan and of how he had opened up to her the previous day. She was glad he had done so, recognising his need to talk. She had even encouraged him to do so, knowing that it would help him. If only she could take her own advice, she thought ruefully as she showered and dressed, but the last thing she wanted to do was to talk about her own problems and she very much doubted it would help to do so anyway. Far better they remained private and firmly locked away in the deepest recesses of her mind.

She had breakfast of orange juice, cereal and toast with Helene and the children then, leaving Helene to take the children to school, she set out for work. It was a beautiful June morning with clear blue skies and warm sunshine, the sort of morning when London sparkled and looked at its very best, but Olivia was only vaguely aware of her surroundings, her mind firmly fixed on the child who had been clinging on so tenuously to life the night before.

Kirstin greeted her as she stepped onto the paediatric unit. 'Olivia…' she began, but that was as far as she got.

'How is she?' Olivia demanded.

'Believe it or not, but she's still holding her own,' said Kirstin. 'I understand there was a very low point around three o'clock this morning but she's rallied again and is stable at the moment.'

'She's unbelievable,' said Olivia, looking towards the HDU. 'Is Sharon still with her?'

'Well, she was, right up until five o'clock, then the staff persuaded her to go and lie down for a couple of hours. She's taking a shower at the moment and is going to go down to the canteen for breakfast. Oh, yes, and Nathan's been in to see Sara as well.'

'Already?' Olivia's eyes widened in surprise.

'He was here just after seven,' said Kirstin. 'I have to say I like the concern he shows for his patients. I get the impression he'll be devastated if Sara doesn't pull through.'

'He will be,' said Olivia. 'There's no doubt about that.'

'And so will you,' observed Kirstin shrewdly.

'Yes, well, Sara and I go back a long way.' Olivia paused. 'I'll go in and see her in a moment.'

'One other thing, Olivia,' said Kirstin, as Olivia would have moved away. 'We have a young boy coming up from A and E shortly. He was involved in an accident last evening—his injuries aren't life-threatening but he's been found to have a seriously irregular heartbeat.'

'All right.' Olivia nodded. 'Let me know when he arrives and I'll come and see him, then, presumably after tests, we'll have to call in Victor Quale to give a definite diagnosis.'

By the time Olivia got in to see Sara, Sharon was back at her daughter's side. She looked hollow-eyed and weary but the light of determination was still in her eyes.

'She's doing well, Dr Gilbert,' she said firmly, when she caught sight of Olivia.

'So I believe,' Olivia replied. Under her mass of tubes and monitors Sara was still locked away in her own silent little world, her eyes closed, her face with its little snub nose turned towards the wall.

'She gave us all a fright,' Sharon went on, 'about three o'clock this morning, but everyone swung into action and within an hour she was stable again.'

Olivia picked up the child's observation chart. It made grim reading but she didn't want to say or do anything to dampen Sharon's amazing optimism in the face of such adversity. On the other hand, neither did she want to raise Sharon's hopes too high in what was increasingly looking to be a deteriorating situation.

'She looks lovely, doesn't she?' she said at last.

'Yes,' Sharon agreed. 'The nurses have just washed her and changed her nightie—that's her favourite one she has on now. And look at this card from her brother and sister— she'll love that with all those animal pictures. I've put it there on her locker so it'll be the first thing she sees when she wakes up.'

Olivia swallowed. 'That's great, Sharon,' she said, then, unable to find anything else to say, she added, 'I'll be back to see you both again later.'

'Yes, all right.' Sharon nodded, then, as if she'd just remembered, she said, 'Sister said Mr Carrington came in earlier to see Sara.'

'Yes, she told me,' said Olivia.

'I think he's lovely,' said Sharon, 'and I know Sara does. She told everyone he is her friend.'

The tears were dangerously prickling the back of Olivia's eyes as she left HDU and made her way back onto the ward.

Throughout the day Sara hovered perilously between life and death, and by the time Olivia had finished her outpatient clinic and returned to the ward to see the new admission, she was still somehow clinging to life.

'Nathan's in there again,' said Kirstin, nodding towards HDU, and even as Olivia turned to look he came out of the unit. As his gaze met hers, her heart seemed to lurch.

'Hello,' she said. It was the first time she'd seen him that day and she was pleased to see that he was looking better than he had the night before. 'How is she now?'

'She's absolutely incredible,' Nathan replied. 'She's still hanging in there. I'm not sure how, but she is.'

'I'm beginning to think her mother's determination not to let her go has something to do with it,' said Olivia.

'Well, whatever it is, it seems to be working,' said Kirstin. 'Now, seeing you are both here, perhaps you'd like to see our new admission. Victor has been in. The boy still needs further tests but it's looking more and more like a heart

valve repair that is needed—so that could be your department, Nathan.'

'Yes, indeed.' Nathan looked around. 'Where is the boy?'

'He's over there in the end bed,' Kirstin replied. As all
three of them began to walk down the ward, she went on, 'His
mother is with him. It's really strange, the boy reminds me of
someone, but for the life of me I can't think who it is.'

They reached the boy's bed, and as he looked up at them
Olivia felt something shift deep inside her, some emotion that
she was at a loss to explain. The boy, who looked to be about
ten years old, had short fair hair, straight dark eyebrows and
grey eyes, and somehow it was the expression in those eyes
that had touched a chord in Olivia. A woman, presumably the
boy's mother, was seated beside the bed with her back to
them, but as the three of them stopped at the foot of the bed
she turned and looked up at them and her gaze met Olivia's.

For Olivia it was one of those extraordinary moments when
the world seemed to stand still, when those around her seemed
to be functioning in slow motion, when everyday sounds
became muffled and life as she knew it seemed to reach a
point of change, as if from that moment onwards things would
never quite be the same again.

Vaguely, through a sudden wave of nausea, she became
aware that Kirstin was speaking. 'This is Drew Jennings,' she
said, 'and his mother, Beverley.' As Kirstin introduced her and
Nathan to the woman and her son, Olivia saw the shock of
recognition in the woman's eyes.

Drawing up every ounce of her professionalism, she
somehow got through the next ten minutes, hopefully asking
the right questions, while Nathan examined the boy until, at
last, she was forced to make her apologies and escape. She

saw Nathan's puzzled but concerned expression just before she fled, and was aware of Kirstin's equally questioning glance, but the one thing that stuck in her mind as she went off duty and left the department was that steady and, oh, so familiar expression in the boy's grey eyes.

Something was very wrong but Nathan couldn't really say what it was. He only knew that Olivia had suddenly and for no apparent reason fled from the ward. He could only assume that she'd suddenly felt ill and yet for some reason he had the feeling there was more to it than that. Kirstin hadn't been able to shed any light on the matter either, saying that Olivia had been perfectly all right prior to that moment. He found himself casting his mind back, trying to ascertain what had happened and why it should have had such an impact on Olivia.

He'd been in to see Sara and on coming out of HDU he'd joined Olivia and Kirstin to go onto the ward to see the new admission—the boy, Drew Jennings, who'd been brought up from A and E. Kirstin had explained the background behind the boy's admission, namely that he'd been in an accident, had suffered minor injuries but that A and E staff had discovered an irregular heartbeat and he'd been admitted to Paediatrics for further investigation.

Up until that point he had been convinced that Olivia had been perfectly all right, so what had happened to change things? Maybe it had simply been that she'd felt suddenly and violently ill, but somehow he still found himself doubting that. He remembered that he'd looked at her and had been startled to see that the colour had drained from her face while the expression in her eyes…well, to coin a phrase, she really had looked as if she'd seen a ghost.

So when had that been? It must have been when they'd reached the boy's bed—but surely that little boy couldn't have upset Olivia to that extent? He'd been a pleasant child, good-looking, if a little serious, but his solemn expression had been transformed when he'd smiled. So, if not the boy, maybe his mother? Had Olivia's strong reaction come about when she'd set eyes on the boy's mother?

The more he thought about it, the more Nathan became convinced that was the case. The woman had turned towards them as they had approached and it had been just after that he'd noticed Olivia's reaction. But who was this woman and why should her presence on the ward have had such an effect on Olivia? She'd seemed quite an ordinary sort of woman, in her thirties, attractive in an understated sort of way, with darkish blonde hair caught up on the top of her head in a clasp and rather prominent blue eyes, but nothing to suggest anything untoward. Which led him to the conclusion that she might be someone of significance from Olivia's past. He'd even found himself going through the boy's records to see if there was any sort of link to Olivia, possibly that she had treated the boy in the past. But there was nothing and he'd finally been forced to admit defeat, but long after he'd gone off duty and returned home he found he couldn't get the incident out of his mind.

He thought about phoning Olivia to see if she was all right, but he suspected that she would say she was even if she wasn't, and that the telephone would be completely inadequate for trying to get to the cause of her distress.

In the end, he decided the only thing to do was to go and see her.

An hour later, in a mood of doubt and apprehension, he

rang her doorbell. He braced himself as he heard the sound of footsteps and someone turning the catch, then the door opened to reveal Helene.

'Mr Carrington!' Her surprise at seeing him was only too apparent.

'Hello, Helene,' he said. 'Is Mrs Gilbert in?'

'No.' Helene shook her head and his heart sank. 'She out walking Oscar—it her turn tonight. You want to come in and wait?'

'That's very kind of you,' Nathan said, 'but actually I think I might go and meet her.'

'OK—she only over in the park.'

'All right, Helene, thanks.'

He turned away then Helene spoke again. 'Mr Carrington?'

'Yes, Helene?' He turned back.

'Mrs Gilbert, she…' Helene hesitated, as if uncertain whether to say more.

'Yes,' he prompted, 'Mrs Gilbert, what?'

'She not good tonight—she upset.' Helene shrugged. 'I not know what is wrong… Perhaps she tell you.'

'Yes, Helene,' he said, 'perhaps she will.'

The evening air was soft and balmy but even that did little to restore Olivia's peace of mind, and as she walked with the faithful Oscar by her side she somehow doubted if she would ever find peace of mind again. Maybe she had been foolish to even imagine that it was over, that it would simply just go away. The fact that she'd heard nothing and that no one had as much as suspected anything in the last two years proved nothing because the situation was still there, very real, and today had proved that it could surface at any time.

The shock at seeing Beverley Jennings again, and this time her son as well, had almost floored her and left her reeling, and even now hours later she still felt decidedly shaky. But she had to face facts. She knew that the boy was in effect her patient, although she knew if she wished she could request that a colleague take over the case. But something deep inside was telling her that she should do this, she should be the one to see the boy's treatment through… But could she do it? Did she have the strength to cope with it?

So lost had she become in her thoughts that she failed to notice the figure walking across the grass to join her. It was only Oscar stopping, wagging his tail and lifting his head in greeting that alerted her. As she turned, her heart seemed to lurch against her ribs. 'Nathan!' she said helplessly. 'What on earth are you doing here?'

'I came to find you,' he said simply. Bending down, he patted Oscar's flank.

'But why…? How did you know I was here?'

'I went to the house,' he said. 'Helene told me you were over here with Oscar.'

'Oh,' she said faintly. 'But why…?'

'Because I was worried about you,' he said. 'You seemed very upset about something at work.'

'Oh,' she said again, and in an attempt to dismiss it, as if it was of little consequence, added, 'It was nothing…really.'

'It didn't seem like nothing from where I was standing,' he said gently. 'In fact, you looked as though you'd seen a ghost.'

'Maybe I had.' She gave a short, false laugh but it had a bitter ring to it. Then, to her horror, she felt a huge lump rise in her throat and tears begin to threaten.

'Do you want to talk about it?' he said, quietly echoing the words she'd said to him only the day before when he'd been so concerned about Jamie.

'I...I'm not sure.' She swallowed.

'You listened to me,' he said, 'and it helped. Maybe it would help you as well.'

'I've never told anyone,' she said slowly, as he fell into step beside her. As the shadows lengthened, they began to stroll together across the grass, with the old dog ambling slowly behind them. 'And to tell you the truth, I would hardly know where to start.'

'I've usually found the beginning is a pretty good place,' he said.

'You're right,' she agreed, 'but I'm not even sure where the beginning is...'

'Then how about going back to the first time you were aware of whatever it is that is troubling you.'

'I don't know...' She shook her head, still reluctant to unburden herself but at the same time strangely almost wanting to do so, to let it all go, to confide in this man, who in the short time that she'd known him had quietly come to fill an important place in her life.

Even as she struggled to find the words, Nathan spoke again. 'Today,' he said, 'on the ward, you seemed distressed to see that boy and his mother—was it anything to do with them?'

'Yes,' she admitted at last, 'it was.'

'Ah,' he said. 'I thought it might be. Would it help if you started by telling me why?'

She took a deep breath. 'The boy,' she said at last, and she spoke so softly that Nathan had to lean towards her to hear what she was saying, 'Drew Jennings—he's Marcus's son.' As she finally spoke the words she was almost amazed to find that nothing dramatic happened but at the same time she felt the tears begin to trickle down her cheeks.

'I see,' said Nathan. 'I wondered if it was something like that.'

'You did?' She looked surprised then, brushing away her tears, she went on, 'It was just such a shock, seeing him like that for the first time…'

'You'd never seen him before?' It was Nathan's turn to show surprise.

'No, never.' She shook her head. 'And…and…I have to say…the thing that shocked me so much was that he is the living image of his father.'

CHAPTER EIGHT

WITHOUT a word Nathan turned and, seeing Olivia's tears, stopped. When she did the same, he stepped towards her and before she had time to think he drew her into his arms. Just for a moment she stiffened and would have pulled away, embarrassed that he should see her like this. But Nathan, it seemed, had other ideas, and even as she attempted to struggle he held her firmly as someone would hold an injured bird making a desperate attempt to escape. And eventually, in the face of such determination, she gave up the attempt and in a sudden wave of exhaustion allowed herself to lean against him as her tears flowed afresh.

Gradually she found she no longer wanted to escape because in the circle of Nathan's arms she felt safe. It had been a very long time since she'd felt this way, and apart from the fleeting comfort of family and friends and that one brief kiss from Nathan it had been a long time since she'd felt a man's arms around her.

They stayed together like that for some considerable time, neither of them talking and with Oscar lying patiently at their feet. Then, very gently, Nathan drew back a little and with one hand tilted her chin so that he could look into her face. Still without speaking, he drew a handkerchief from his pocket and tenderly wiped away her tears.

'I think,' he said at last, 'we should go back to the house, then you can tell me what happened.'

Suddenly, and to her surprise, she found she wanted to do just that. 'Yes, all right,' she whispered.

'You'll feel much better afterwards,' he said softly, then, leaning forward, he kissed her. Her breath caught in her throat at the touch of his lips but even as she was wondering just how she should respond he drew away. Taking her hand and tucking it through his arm, he whistled to Oscar and they set off across the park.

'So how did you first become aware of this boy's existence?' It was much later, after Olivia and Nathan had returned to the house. The children were in bed, Helene was in her rooms and they were seated in Olivia's sitting room, Nathan in a deep comfortable armchair and Olivia opposite him on the sofa.

'It was his mother I became aware of first,' Olivia replied. She was feeling more composed now and had poured a glass of wine for Nathan and one for herself.

'And when was that?' he asked.

'I first saw her at Marcus's funeral,' she said, and there was a slight tremor in her voice.

'And did you know about her before then?' Nathan frowned.

'No.' She shook her head. 'Nothing.'

He stared at her as if he could hardly believe what she was saying. 'So…how did you know who she was?'

'I didn't…not then,' she said. 'I must admit, I got through that day as if I was in a dream. I saw this woman at the church and later at the cemetery, where she left a bunch of flowers.

She seemed very upset and I remember wondering briefly who she was. I think at the time I simply thought she was another of Marcus's colleagues—there were so many of them there, some I knew and some I didn't, but most of them came back here afterwards.'

'And this woman didn't?'

'No, she didn't and, well, I suppose I simply forgot about her—it was a very difficult time for us all.'

'I can imagine,' Nathan murmured.

She was silent for a moment, struggling with her emotions. 'I loved Marcus so much, you see,' she said quietly at last, and once again her voice faltered. 'We met at a party and I suppose you could say it was one of those love-at-first-sight affairs. I hadn't believed in them until then—but, well, it happened and we had a whirlwind romance and we were married within a year.'

'And you were happy?'

'Oh, yes,' she said quickly, then a shadow seemed to cross her features. 'At least, I thought we were,' she added, and there was a touch of bitterness now. 'Marcus was doing very well by this time and had just become a partner in a law firm in the Temple. I gave up work for a time when Charlotte was born but after a year I went back to St Benedict's on a part-time basis, and the same thing happened when Lewis was born two years later. We were so fortunate…we had a wonderful lifestyle… It was terrible when Marcus was killed—I really thought my world had ended.'

'You said it was a road crash,' he said.

'Yes,' she said. 'He went out one night. He said he was going to his mother's in Eastbourne, but the crash happened in Milton Keynes, which I now know is where Beverley

Jennings lives…' She trailed off, unable for the moment to continue as for the first time she began to put into words exactly what had happened.

'So how did you find out in the end?' asked Nathan gently.

'She came to see me,' Olivia replied, her voice flat now.

'What here—to the house?' He raised his eyebrows.

'Yes, I recognised her as the woman from the funeral as soon as I opened the door. She said she wanted to talk to me— I asked her in and it was then that she told me. She said that she and Marcus had known one another since they were children. Marcus's parents were very well off in those days—they owned a large country estate in Berkshire and Beverley's parents were employed on the estate. She told me they went out together for a time but that Marcus's parents soon put a stop to it because she said they didn't think she was good enough for their son. Anyway, Marcus eventually went off to university and they didn't see each other again for a long time. They apparently met up again about eleven years ago…'

'Before he met you?'

'Yes,' Olivia agreed, 'before he met me. According to her, they had an on-and-off affair and she became pregnant. That was a real shock, I can tell you. It certainly didn't surprise me that Marcus had had other girlfriends before he met me, but I never imagined he'd fathered a child and kept that from me.'

'But surely he didn't continue to see this woman after he'd met you?' Nathan frowned.

'Not at first,' she said. 'She told me that after he met me he told her that they mustn't see one another again.'

'But had he acknowledged the child?'

'Oh, yes. Marcus's name is on the child's birth certificate and apparently he was paying maintenance for him.'

'Did he see the boy?'

'Not at first, but then she said…they met by chance one day in the street and after that he began visiting the boy…and then—and I think this is the hardest part of all—some time later they resumed their affair.'

'And do you know when that would have been?'

'I'm not sure exactly.' Olivia shook her head, clearly distressed. 'But I think just after Lewis was born. I simply couldn't believe it, and for months after she'd told me, I would find myself going over and over it in my mind, remembering different things that I'd shared with Marcus. You know the sort of thing—birthdays, Christmas celebrations, holidays—times that I thought had been so precious to me and to us as a family, when all the time…he was seeing her. Do you know?' She stared at Nathan. 'In the end I even found myself thinking that this sense of betrayal was worse than the actual grief of losing Marcus. That might seem a dreadful thing to say, but it's true. I had started to cope with the grief, partly I think because I was secure in the knowledge that I had been truly loved by Marcus. But then finding out this, well, it's been terrible—can you believe that?'

'Oh, yes,' said Nathan quietly. Leaning forward, he rested his arms on his knees and loosely linked his hands. 'I can certainly believe it. Being betrayed by someone you loved and someone you thought loved only you is one of the most devastating feelings there is.'

'Oh.' Olivia stared at him. 'I'm sorry, I'd forgotten—you know all about this, don't you?'

He nodded. 'Yes, Susan left me for another man…so, yes, to a certain extent I really do know how you felt and I can sympathise with you. But let's forget my situation, it's you we're talking about.' He paused. 'You said you thought Marcus loved you,' he went on after a moment, 'and from what you've told me, I would say he most certainly did. He'd known this woman for a long time before he'd met you and had fathered her child. He should have told you about it but he didn't. It sounds like he coped with it until he actually saw the boy. I guess at that time his paternal instincts kicked in…'

'Yes, and I can understand that, but what I can't understand, and what I find so difficult to forgive, is why he resumed the affair…'

'Who knows?' Nathan shrugged. 'You say they had a long history—that in itself can be a very powerful factor. He was also visiting the boy by then. Maybe at the time it happened he'd been having a bad day. It's no excuse, I know,' he added hastily, when Olivia looked up sharply, 'but it could be a reason. You say you think it was just after Lewis was born—maybe you'd been having bad nights, maybe the two of you hadn't had sex for some time—I don't know. Again, it's no excuse for his behaviour, but what I think I'm trying to show you is that it sounds as if the set of circumstances your husband found himself caught up in was probably entirely separate from his feelings for you and indeed from his whole life with you and the children.'

Olivia was silent for a long moment then slowly she said, 'I must admit I'd never looked at it like that before…'

'And, of course, the other thing I think you need to remember is that you only have this woman's word for it that the affair was actually resumed.'

'But if it wasn't, why would he have been visiting her?'

'Simply to see his son?'

Helplessly, Olivia stared at him. 'I don't know, Nathan,' she said at last. 'I really don't know…'

'And probably you never will know, but what you haven't told me is why she came to see you when she did—although I think I can guess the answer to that one.'

'Money,' said Olivia flatly.

'I thought as much.' Nathan nodded. 'If your husband had been paying maintenance to her, presumably on his death it stopped abruptly.'

'Yes, it did. She came to see me when the details of Marcus's estate were published. I was really angry at first and didn't want to believe any of it, but she had brought the boy's birth certificate with her and some other documentation, which proved that he was Marcus's son.'

'Had Marcus mentioned the boy in his will?'

'No, he hadn't.' Olivia sighed. 'But once I'd calmed down a bit I knew in my heart he wouldn't have wanted the boy to suffer hardship.'

'So what did you do?' Nathan sounded faintly incredulous now.

'Well, I knew there was no way I could keep up the maintenance payments...Marcus had left us reasonably well off but I'd had to return to full-time work and Marcus's mother had even offered to pay Helene's wages so that I was able to remain in this house. So...so... I gave her a one-off payment from the life insurance I'd taken out on Marcus.'

Nathan stared at her. 'That was incredibly generous of you. Did she threaten you in any way—blackmail or anything like that?'

Olivia shook her head. 'No, nothing like that. I think she just wanted what she felt was her son's due and, in fairness, I think she really was finding life a bit of a struggle. If she had threatened me by saying she would make details of her relationship with Marcus public, I would have had to let her do so, even though I dreaded all this coming out.'

'And has she come back to you for more money?'

'No.' Olivia shook her head again. 'I had my solicitor draw up the details of the payment and I have to say I never heard any more from her.'

'Until today,' said Nathan softly.

'Until today,' Olivia agreed. 'And like I said before, the biggest shock today was seeing Drew, and recognising his likeness to Marcus. If there had ever been any doubt in my mind before, it vanished in that instant.'

'Have you really never told anyone else about any of this?'

'No.' Olivia swallowed. 'I couldn't bear the thought of anyone else knowing. Everyone thought Marcus and I were so happy...'

'And you were...'

'They thought he was a loving husband and father and... Oh, I don't know, but I really couldn't bear the thought of telling people—his family, my family, our friends...'

'Do you think this woman has said anything at the hospital?'

'I don't know.' Olivia shrugged helplessly. 'I don't even know if the boy knows who I am...'

'He didn't appear to know anything about you,' said Nathan slowly, 'but, on the other hand, did his mother know you worked at St Benedict's? Could she have been expecting to see you?'

'I don't know the answer to that either,' Olivia replied. 'I thought she seemed as surprised to see me as I was to see her. The other thing I've agonised over is why the boy was brought to St Benedict's when they live in Milton Keynes.'

'Didn't Kirstin say he'd been admitted from A and E, that

he was involved in some sort of accident? Perhaps they were simply on a day out in London.'

'Maybe. I just don't know.' She shook her head. 'But you mentioning Kirstin, that's another thing…'

'What do you mean? I thought you said no one else knows.'

'They don't, but Kirstin was going on about how the boy reminded her of someone—it may be only a matter of time before it clicks and she realises he is the image of Marcus.'

'Would it really be so terrible if people knew?' he said softly.

'I don't know,' she said, and her voice was suddenly weary. 'I don't know about anything any more…'

'Mummy…?' Suddenly a little voice from the doorway made them both turn to find Charlotte in her nightie standing in the open doorway, looking uncertainly from Olivia to Nathan then back to Olivia again.

'Darling, what is it?' Olivia held out her hand to her daughter, who after only a further moment's hesitation ran across the room and clambered onto her mother's lap.

'I woke up. I heard talking,' she said. Looking across at Nathan from beneath her lashes, she went on, 'Voices… I thought…I thought it was…Daddy.'

'Oh, darling.' Olivia put her arms around the little girl and buried her face in her hair. After a moment she said, 'Mr Carrington came to see me. We've just been…talking.'

'What have you been talking about?' mumbled Charlotte.

'Actually,' said Olivia, with a quick glance at Nathan, 'we were talking about Daddy.'

'Were you?' Charlotte sounded surprised then after a long pause she said, 'But he's not going to come back—is he?'

'No, darling, he isn't,' Olivia replied, her voice compassionate but at the same time firm. She was just wondering whether she should say anything further when Charlotte spoke again, this time lifting her head and looking fully at Nathan. 'I had a card from Jamie today,' she said.

'Did you?' Nathan looked surprised.

'Yes, he sent me a picture of his school—he said he would. Can I send him a picture of my school, Mummy?'

'Of course you can,' Olivia replied. 'But talking of school, you'd better get back to bed now otherwise you'll never be up in the morning. Come on, I'll come and tuck you in. I'll be back in a minute, Nathan.'

When she returned to the sitting room, after settling Charlotte in her bed, Nathan was on his feet. 'Oh,' she said, 'are you going?'

'I think I should.' Moving towards her, he said, 'But, please, don't worry any more, Olivia, everything will be all right. And I've been thinking. If you wanted, you could pass this boy's treatment over to Hugh Jefferson.'

'I know I could,' she agreed. 'I did think about it but in a strange sort of way I ended up thinking it was something I should do—can you understand that?' By this time Nathan was standing directly in front of her and as she spoke she looked up into his face.

'Yes,' he said slowly, 'I think I can, but if you feel you can't, it isn't too late to change your mind.' He paused, his gaze searching her features. 'I'm glad you told me,' he added after a moment.

'Yes,' she said, 'so am I. I feel quite a sense of relief at having shared it. Thank you for listening, Nathan.'

'Oh, Olivia.' He looked down into her eyes. 'It was the very least I could do.'

With a deep sigh he reached out and for the second time

that day drew her into his arms. This time his kiss was firm and decisive and for Olivia there was no confusion over how she should act. This time her response was purely spontaneous, her lips parting beneath his, her arms around his shoulders, her fingers sinking into his hair. It felt good, very, very good—no, more than that, it felt exciting as the almost forgotten coil of desire began to unwind deep inside her, unleashing passions she had despaired of ever feeling again.

And then, all too soon, it was over and Nathan was drawing away, his expression one of almost rueful surprise, as if what he had expected to be yet another chaste, friendly kiss had escalated into something very much more, something that carried with it a promise of even greater delight to come.

'I think…' he murmured shakily, 'I really had better go…'

Later, much later, long after Nathan had gone, she lay in her bed wide awake, gazing up at the ceiling and going over and over in her mind the events of the day. She had no regrets at telling Nathan what had happened after Marcus's death, and in a strange sort of way that which she had dreaded for so long hadn't seemed such a big deal after all. Nathan had seemed to bring such a sense of calm common sense to the whole situation that she had almost ended up wondering why she had allowed herself to suffer so much torment and agony in the past two years. Maybe it would have been better if she could have faced the situation head on and told her close family and friends about Marcus's other, secret life, but she had chosen not to and had consequently suffered alone.

And now she'd told Nathan and the relief was enormous, but even that seemed now to be paling into insignificance in the face of this new situation that appeared to be growing between Nathan and herself. If anyone had told her—and several had tried—she would never have believed that she was ready to embark on a new relationship and, really, if she was honest, she hadn't intended to actually embark on this. Oh, she'd found him attractive, she couldn't deny that. From that very first moment when she'd caught sight of him across Claudia's drawing room she'd been attracted, but she'd imagined that was as far as it would go. She'd always doubted she could love anyone as much as she'd once loved Marcus, and since learning of his betrayal she'd never imagined she could trust anyone again. But somehow Nathan was different. He, too, was vulnerable; he too knew what it was to be betrayed by someone who had meant the world to him. But, she reminded herself in the small hours of the night, he also had implied that he wasn't interested in starting another relationship, that he would also maybe find it difficult to place his trust again. So perhaps caution was required here.

With that thought uppermost in her mind, Olivia finally attempted to sleep, but her very last conscious thoughts were not of caution or betrayal but of the utter sweetness and excitement she'd found in Nathan's kiss.

He was falling in love with her—Nathan knew that without the shadow of a doubt. He hadn't meant to, even though there was no denying he'd been captivated by her since that very first moment when he'd caught sight of her in Rory and Claudia's garden. But a full-scale relationship had been the last thing on his mind and what seemed to be happening now between the two of them had crept up on him and taken him unawares.

Until now he hadn't really believed he would be able to fully trust a woman again, not after Susan, but that had been before he'd met Olivia and since then, he had to admit, nothing had quite been the same again.

He'd felt almost honoured that she'd chosen to tell him about her late husband, and while part of him had felt anger at the way Marcus had treated her, he hoped he'd been able to help her to see events from a slightly different perspective.

He knew the coming days at St Benedict's could prove difficult for Olivia as she dealt with Drew Jennings but he hoped, now that he knew the full story, he would be able to give her the support she so badly needed.

The following morning, after a night where Olivia had filled his dreams, Nathan arrived at St Benedict's, bracing himself to receive the news he'd been dreading on Sara Middleton. But far from finding a ward filled with mourning, he was delighted and relieved to find that not only had Sara survived another night but that she was also showing definite signs of improvement.

'It's nothing short of a miracle really,' said Kirstin. 'In fact, she's doing so well that we should be able to move her out of HDU and back onto the main ward in the next day or so.'

'That's the kind of news I like to hear,' said Nathan, reading through Sara's notes. His spirits, already high from his meeting with Olivia the night before, now seemed to soar.

'Needless to say, Sharon is ecstatic,' said Kirstin, 'but having said that, I don't really think there was a moment when she didn't think Sara would pull through. And Olivia, of course, is delighted as well, although she was a little more realistic and accepted the high risk factor that Sara faced.'

'Yes, quite,' Nathan agreed, then with an almost nonchalant glance around the ward, which he feared didn't for one moment fool Kirstin, he went on, 'Er…is Olivia around?'

'Yes.' Kirstin smiled. 'She came in to see Sara, and now she's gone to Special Care to see baby William Munns.'

'Oh, right. Well, maybe I should go down there as well,' said Nathan, 'before I go to Theatre. It's time I checked up on the little chap,' he added hastily.

'Of course.' Kirstin's expression was inscrutable.

'And what about the new boy—Drew Jennings?'

Kirstin nodded. 'He had a good night. We're just awaiting his test results then Dr Quale will make his decision regarding any surgery that may be needed.'

'Right,' Nathan said. Then, curiously, he went on, 'What address do we have for Drew?'

'Address?' Kirstin frowned. 'Wait a minute. I have his notes here. Let me see. Oh, yes, it's a Putney address.'

'Putney? Oh, right, I see. Thanks, Kirstin,' he said, but as he would have moved away, Kirstin spoke again.

'Is there a problem with that?' she asked curiously.

'No, not at all. I just wondered, that's all.' He made his escape before Kirstin became too inquisitive. She already seemed to have some intuition as to his relationship with Olivia, although he doubted that even she knew just how far that had progressed, but he certainly didn't want her to learn from him of Olivia's involvement with Drew Jennings.

On his way to Special Care he found his anticipation mounting at the thought of seeing Olivia for the first time since the precious moments they'd shared the night before. He felt a sharp stab of excitement at the very thought of it. He'd been cautious, to say the least, afraid not only of rushing Olivia into something she wasn't ready for or even didn't want but also of not wanting her to think that he was using her vulnerability and the situation she had just confided to him as a means to further his own interests.

But he'd received a shock because while he'd been expecting a repeat of those other occasions—at her home after supper and in the park, when he had kissed her—a soft, gentle touching of lips in what had been a comforting embrace from him, this latest time had been totally different. This time Olivia had responded with a passion that had sent his senses into freefall in a kiss that had left him wanting her with a desire stronger than anything he'd experienced for years. In the end he'd been compelled to draw away, frightened he'd been about to disgrace himself completely by letting her know just how much he wanted her. And now he was about to see her again.

Taking a deep breath, he entered the essentially unique world of the special care baby unit and went through the required scrubbing-up routine. Rosemary Morris was on duty and she escorted him onto the main ward. 'You're William's second visitor this morning.' She smiled. 'Olivia's with him at the moment.'

'Really?' murmured Nathan, as if he'd had no idea that Olivia was even in the vicinity, which, given the thumping of his heart as they entered the ward, was quite a difficult thing to do.

She was standing by the cot, with baby William cradled in her arms, her expression infinitely tender as the baby's parents, Julie and Dave, looked on. She looked utterly adorable in her tunic and trousers, and even though that glorious hair was tucked away inside a cap it only seemed to accentuate the fineness of her profile and the delicate arch of her eyebrows. She must have sensed Nathan and Rosemary's approach for she half turned and then—what? What was that expression in those lovely dark eyes as they met his? Was it pleasure, or surprise, or a mixture of both? Was it tinged with the memory of what they had shared or was he imagining it all? Was she merely just acknowledging the presence of a colleague?

'Nathan,' she said. 'So you've also come to see just how well William is doing.'

'I have indeed,' he replied, and he was amazed at how normal his voice sounded. 'And I like what I see.' He smiled at Julie Munns.

'He's doing so well,' said Julie, 'and it's all thanks to you and this wonderful team here.' As she spoke, the baby opened his eyes, waved his tiny fists in the air and began to kick.

'Glad to be of service,' said Nathan with a chuckle. 'Any problems at all, Olivia?'

'Not really,' Olivia replied. 'His breathing is good now and he's feeding well—isn't that right, Rosemary?'

'Yes, indeed.' Rosemary nodded. She took the baby from Olivia and placed him back inside his cot, covering him with a soft blue blanket. 'I would say probably another couple of weeks on the unit then we could talk about him going home.'

'You hear that, Dave?' There were tears in Julie's eyes as she turned to her husband. He was so overcome, he was totally unable to speak.

Ten minutes later Nathan and Olivia left the special unit together. 'Are you all right?' he said, throwing her a side-long glance.

'Yes,' she replied, 'I'm fine, but I want to thank you, Nathan.'

'Whatever for?' he said softly. Suddenly he had to fight an overwhelming urge to gather her up into his arms right there in the corridor.

'For everything,' she said. 'For listening to me, for under-standing and for being there for me.'

'Not at all,' he said gruffly. 'And I shall go on being there for you, I want you to know that.'

'Thank you,' she whispered.

'Have you seen Drew Jennings yet this morning?' he asked after a moment.

'No, not yet,' she replied. 'I'm going back there now.'

'Do you want me to come with you?' he asked.

'No, Nathan, thank you.' She shook her head. 'This is something I have to do for myself.'

'You've decided to take his case, then?' he said.

'I think so,' she said. 'It rather depends on his mother's attitude towards me, but I'll let you know what I decide.'

'Just one thing,' said Nathan, 'did you know they've given their address as Putney?'

'Really?' Olivia stopped and stared at him. 'Not Milton Keynes?'

'No, not Milton Keynes.'

'That's interesting,' she said. 'They must have moved.'

'I wonder why,' he mused.

'I don't know.' She shrugged. 'Maybe I'll find out when I talk to them.'

'I have to go into Theatre shortly,' he said, 'but I'll be around later if you need me.'

'Thanks, Nathan,' she said again. 'I doubt I could get through this without you.'

'Don't mention it.' They'd stopped by this time at the entrance to the paediatric ward, and for a long moment they simply stood in silence, looking at one another. Then, in an attempt to calm the tide of emotion that threatened to overwhelm him, Nathan said, 'Was Charlotte all right last night—about me being there, I mean?'

'Yes, she was fine,' Olivia replied. 'It was just that she woke up and I suppose hearing a man's voice, which is pretty unusual in our household these days, in her sleepy state she thought it was Marcus.'

'Poor little girl,' said Nathan.

'I know. She misses him terribly, but once she'd got over her mistake she was absolutely fine about you being there.'

'Well, I'm glad about that.' Nathan smiled and would have said more but at that moment the door opened and Kirstin suddenly appeared.

'Oh,' she said, looking speculatively from one to the other of them, 'what are you two doing out here? I almost tripped over you.'

'We were just talking, that's all,' said Olivia.

'Of course you were,' said Kirstin sweetly, then before either of them could say anything further she put her head in the air and waltzed off down the corridor.

'I'd better go,' said Nathan almost sheepishly.

'And me,' Olivia replied. 'See you later.'

With that she was gone into the ward, leaving Nathan to make his way to Theatre, sorry that he wouldn't be seeing more of her, at least for the time being, but at the same time elated at the look that had been in her eyes when she'd first caught sight of him.

CHAPTER NINE

'HELLO, Drew,' said Olivia, as she sat down beside the boy's bed.

'Hello,' he said, looking up from the comic he was reading.

'Just thought we might have a little chat.' Olivia realised as she looked at the boy in front of her that not only did she have to contend with his likeness to her late husband but also fleeting likenesses in colouring and characteristics to both of her own children.

'What about?' he said warily.

'Nothing much.' Olivia gave a little shrug. 'Are you happy in here, Drew?'

'Suppose so. I'd rather go home, though. I didn't really hurt myself that much when I came off my bike, but when I came in here they said there's something wrong with my heart and that I might have to have an operation. What I can't understand is why I have to stay here. If there was something wrong with my heart before I came in here and I was OK at home, I don't see why I can't go home until they decide what they are going to do.'

The boy's logic, which was so reminiscent of Marcus's astute powers of reasoning, took Olivia's breath away. 'It's better that you do stay here for the time being, Drew,' she said at last. 'The thing is,' she went on quickly, when he would have opened his mouth to argue some more, 'if we had known about your heart condition before you had your accident, we would have had you in here pretty sharpish.' She paused. 'Is your mum coming in today?'

He nodded. 'Yes, she'll be in later—she helps Matt in the garage.'

'Matt?' said Olivia.

'He's her boyfriend,' Drew explained, then added with breathtaking candour, 'But he's not my father.'

'Oh, really?' Olivia tried hard not to show undue interest but suddenly she needed to know what was happening in the life of this boy and his mother.

'No,' said Drew. 'My father died.'

'I'm sorry to hear that,' she said.

'He was killed in a car crash two years ago.'

'You must miss him very much,' Olivia heard herself say.

'Yeah, I do…all the time.' The boy's face suddenly clouded over, and as it dawned on Olivia that he had suffered just as much as Charlotte and Lewis, her heart went out to him. 'He didn't live with us,' he went on, and Olivia knew she should stop him but something prevented her and in growing fascination she knew she wanted to hear what he had to say. 'He had another family,' he said. 'He used to come and see us when he could. I wished he'd stay all the time but he told me he couldn't, he said his other children needed him as well.'

'These other children—did you ever see them?' She asked the question then held her breath, not knowing how she would cope if Drew said that, yes, he had seen Charlotte and Lewis, that Marcus had taken them to meet him, maybe when they had been little more than toddlers.

'No.' He shook his head and Olivia breathed again. 'But he showed me a picture of them,' he added.

'Did he?' she said faintly.

'Yes, he said I should know what they look like because they were my half-sister and -brother.'

Olivia drew in her breath sharply—this was an aspect she'd never even considered before.

'Mum was upset when Dad died,' Drew went on, oblivious to the turmoil Olivia was going through. 'I didn't think she was ever going to stop crying.'

'Oh,' said Olivia faintly, then, in an effort to shift the emphasis, not wanting to hear of Beverley's pain, she said, 'But you are both feeling better now?'

'Yeah, I s'ppose so,' he said.

'Your…your mum has…Matt?'

He nodded. 'Yes, we met him at the bowling alley one day.' He shrugged. 'And he's been around ever since. We live with him now,' he added casually.

Olivia took a deep breath, 'And do you like him, Drew?' she asked. Suddenly it was terribly important to her that he should.

'Yeah.' He grinned, Marcus's grin, and her heart lurched painfully. 'He's dead cool…and he takes me to watch Spurs play.'

'Well.' She stood up. 'That's really good.'

'So when are you going to do this operation?' he said, looking up at her.

'Just as soon as we can,' she replied. 'Now, you get some rest and I'll have a word with your mum when she comes in to see you.'

'He's a little cracker, isn't he?' said Kirstin, as Olivia joined her in her office. 'Drew, that is,' she added, when Olivia frowned.

'Oh, yes. Yes, he is,' she agreed.

'Who did you think I meant—Nathan?' said Kirstin with a grin.

'Now, why would I think that?' In spite of herself, Olivia felt her cheeks grow warm.

'Oh, come on, Olivia.' Kirstin was never one to pull her punches. 'It's blatantly obvious what's going on between the two of you.'

'I don't know what on earth you mean,' Olivia replied primly.

'Yes, you do,' Kirstin retorted. 'You're all of a twitter whenever he's around…'

'I'm not!' she protested, but Kirstin ignored her.

'While Nathan—why, it's obvious to anyone that he fancies you rotten.'

'Don't be silly,' said Olivia firmly, but deep inside there was a warm glow in the region of her heart.

'Who's being silly?' Kirstin shrugged. 'What does it matter, for heaven's sake? If it's happening, just enjoy it. You deserve it—it's about time you had someone else to care for you. Now, getting back to Drew—is he your patient or Hugh Jefferson's?'

'Most probably he'll be mine,' said Olivia, 'but I want to speak to his mother when she comes in.'

'All right.' Kirstin looked a little bemused but she didn't comment further. In the next couple of hours the ward became such a hive of activity, with children being admitted, two being discharged and another going to Theatre, that there was no chance for further speculation.

Olivia eventually returned to her own consulting room where she and Trudy completed a large pile of correspondence. Not surprisingly, she found it difficult to concentrate with all that was taking place in her life. Her talk with Drew had put an almost eerie perspective on the situation as it had gradually dawned on her just how much he, too, had been affected by Marcus's death. His mother also must have been equally affected, but that was an aspect she couldn't bring herself to even contemplate. She'd been surprised, but at the same time unsure why she was surprised, firstly that she had liked Drew so much and secondly that there was a new man in the lives of his mother and himself. Maybe Kirstin was right, she thought with a little smile, and it really was time to move on, not just for her but for everyone who had been involved in Marcus's life.

But was Kirstin right in her other theory, over the way that Nathan felt about her? She really wasn't sure, she only knew that for her own part she felt a frisson of excitement every time he appeared. How he really felt about her, however, was anyone's guess.

'Olivia.' She looked up sharply and realised that she'd become so lost in her thoughts that she hadn't realised that Trudy was talking to her.

'Oh, Trudy, I'm sorry, I was miles away. What is it?' As she spoke she saw that Trudy was holding the telephone receiver.

'It's Kirstin,' said Trudy. 'She says to tell you that Ms Jennings has just arrived on the ward?'

'Oh, right.' Olivia felt her stomach churn. 'Tell her I'll be right there.'

She allowed herself a moment to compose herself before this meeting with the woman who had apparently meant so much to her husband. Going into her cloakroom, she checked her make-up and combed her hair, then smoothing down the jacket of her navy pin-striped suit, she took a deep breath and left her office.

On the last occasion they had met, when Beverley had come to the house, she had decidedly had the upper hand over Olivia, who at that time had barely known of her existence, let alone the part she'd played in Marcus's life. This time the cards were stacked in her favour; this time Beverley was just another anxious mother seeking reassurance over her sick child.

Olivia found her sitting in the relatives' room, nervously twisting her hands together. She would have stood up when Olivia came into the room but Olivia stopped her, instead taking a seat herself. 'Hello, Beverley.' She came straight to the point, noting as she did so that her use of the woman's first name seemed to ease the tension in the room. 'How are you?'

'I'm OK…' Beverley hesitated. 'And you?' She looked tired and drawn, her hair pulled back from her face and fastened with a clasp.

'I'm fine.' Olivia nodded briskly. 'I've spoken to Drew today,' she went on, but before she could continue Beverley looked up sharply.

'You haven't told him?' she said.

'Told him what?' Olivia frowned.

'Well, who you are?'

'No, of course not.' Olivia shook her head then, seeing Beverley's look of relief, she went on, 'I can't see it would serve any purpose at the present time.'

'No.' Beverley shook her head. 'I think…he's just starting to get over it…'

'Marcus's death, you mean?' said Olivia, and as she spoke she saw that her directness surprised Beverley.

'Yes,' Beverley said, then, taking a deep breath, she went on, 'That, and the fact that our lives have changed recently. I've met someone else, you see…'

'Drew told me,' said Olivia. Beverley looked up sharply and she added, 'He volunteered the information. He also said you'd moved to London to live and that he thought that—Matt, isn't it?—is dead cool. I think was the expression he used.'

The ghost of a smile crossed Beverley's features. 'Yes,' she said, 'they get on really well. Matt's been so good for Drew—he needed a man around…' She trailed off then anxiously she looked up and Olivia saw the gleam of tears in her eyes, 'He…he is going to be all right, isn't he?'

'He needs surgery, Beverley, to correct this leaking valve in his heart, but it's quite a straightforward procedure and we have the very best cardiac team here at St Benedict's so, please, try not to worry.'

'I…I…didn't know you worked here,' said Beverley after a moment. 'I knew you were a doctor, of course, but not where you worked. When Drew was brought up here from A and E I was as surprised to see you as you must have been to see me.'

'Yes,' Olivia admitted, 'it was a shock, but we have to put that to one side now. Drew is what is important, his condition and his treatment, which we hope will lead to a complete recovery. Now, as soon as we have a date for his operation and we know who will be carrying out his surgery, I will come and talk through the whole procedure with you, but for the time being, I think you need to just go and be with Drew and keep him as relaxed and happy as possible.'

'Yes, all right.' Beverley stood up and walked a little shakily to the door, where she turned and looked at Olivia. 'Thank you, Dr Gilbert,' she said quietly. 'Thank you so much.'

Olivia saw Nathan briefly later that day. He was coming out of Theatre still dressed in his green scrubs, his hair damp, almost spiky from where he'd been wearing his cap. He looked tired but his expression brightened when he caught sight of her.

'Hello,' she said, casually, she hoped, but at the same time fearful that he must be aware of the way her pulse was racing or, if not that, then surely he must be able to hear her heart hammering. 'I'm glad I've seen you.'

'Me, too,' he murmured, and at the look in his eyes she felt the colour rush to her cheeks.

'I…I wanted to tell you,' she said. 'I've decided to take Drew Jennings as my patient.'

'I'm glad,' he said softly.

'It was just something I felt I had to do.'

'I'd hoped you'd reach that conclusion,' he replied, then after a pause he said, 'Have you spoken to his mother?'

'Yes, I have. I saw her after I'd spoken to Drew. She has a new man in her life…she and Drew have moved in with him.'

'Hence the move to Putney…'

'Yes, hence the move to Putney.'

'Well, I guess life goes on.' He paused. 'Did it upset you, talking to them?'

'Actually, no, it didn't.' She shook her head. 'I wasn't looking forward to it—but you already know that.' She waved her hand dismissively. 'But it was strange. I told you that Drew bears a strong resemblance to Marcus, didn't I? Well, it wasn't only that I was aware of while I was talking to him, it was also the likeness to Charlotte and Lewis—Charlotte especially—and in the end all I could think was not what Marcus had or hadn't done but that this little boy is sick and needs our help, and how I might feel if it was one of my own children lying there in that bed.'

'Good for you,' he murmured. 'But speaking of that, have you spoken to Victor yet?'

'Yes, I have, and he's given the go-ahead for an immediate mitral valve repair. As it happens, there's been a cancellation in tomorrow's list so Drew has been slotted in there.'

'That'll be me, then,' said Nathan. 'Richard Parker will be in Manchester.'

'I'm glad it's you,' said Olivia. 'Will you come with me and explain the procedure to Drew and his mother?'

'Of course I will. Let me change out of these togs and I'll be right with you.'

Nathan's heart ached for Olivia. It couldn't be easy for her in the bizarre situation she now found herself, and he made up his mind that he would do all he could to help her to cope. It was the following morning and Nathan's first waking thoughts had been of Olivia. He had gone with her the day before to talk to Beverley Jennings and her son and explain the procedure he would use to repair the boy's heart valve.

Matt had also been present and he'd been so full of concern for the boy that in a strange sort of way Nathan had found himself thinking that had helped Olivia to cope with the situation. He knew that the whole episode with Drew had brought back the circumstances of Marcus's death and his relationship with Beverley with frightening clarity, but he had also found himself hoping that it might be the catalyst that was required to allow Olivia to move on with her life. And the more he thought about that, the more convinced he became that he wanted to be the one who would help her to do just that.

He was over Susan—he was sure of that now. He hadn't

been until he'd met Olivia but she had given him hope that there was indeed a life beyond Susan, just as he hoped he'd helped Olivia to realise there was a life beyond Marcus.

The very thought of that future filled him with excitement. That there would be problems to overcome he had no doubt, the greatest of these being that they had three children between them and he knew that Charlotte and Lewis's happiness would be of paramount importance to Olivia in any future plans, just as Jamie's would be to him. But, even in the face of all that, he was certain that they would be able to work things out—at least the children liked each other, he thought ruefully as he prepared to leave for work.

It was the morning of Drew's operation and he felt confident and elated, but as he stepped out of his apartment block the heavens opened and the sudden deluge seemed to have a sobering effect on his enthusiasm. Maybe he was jumping the gun, he thought, thinking about the future in such a way. Maybe Olivia wasn't interested in him in that way at all— maybe it was all in his imagination.

His thoughts raced on as he ran for the tube. Surely there had been some indication from Olivia that she felt the same way as he did? Surely there was some significance in the way she looked at him and if not in that, then what about the way she had kissed him? He hadn't imagined that.

But as he collapsed onto a seat in a corner of a tube carriage, he told himself firmly that really there was only one way to put paid to his fears and anxieties and that was to ask Olivia how she felt. Perhaps now the time had come to find out just what the path ahead was to be. Yes, that was it—after Drew's operation today he would ask Olivia out. It was time, he told himself firmly. He'd held back for long enough fearful that

Olivia wasn't yet ready, but he couldn't go on like that for ever. Now was the time to move things forward.

He must have been smiling to himself, or maybe he had laughed out loud at the prospect of furthering his relationship with Olivia, he didn't know, but when he looked up it was to find that a middle-aged lady on the other side of the carriage was giving him a very strange look indeed.

Olivia had long felt that the atmosphere in Theatre was like no other—highly charged, sometimes tense with drama but always with a calm sense of efficiency and professionalism that was unique. She had stayed with Beverley after Drew's pre-med then accompanied them to the anaesthetic room, where Diana took over.

'He'll be fine,' she said to Beverley. 'I'll come and find you when it's all over. Is Matt staying with you?'

'Yes, he's in the relatives' room,' Beverley replied.

'Melanie will go with you.' Olivia nodded towards Staff Nurse Melanie Thorpe, who had accompanied Drew and the porters to the theatre.

Beverley turned to go then she stopped. 'Dr Gilbert,' she said, and Olivia turned back.

'Yes?' She raised her eyebrows.

'Thank you again,' said Beverley.

'Whatever for?' Olivia tried to maintain the matter-of-fact manner she had adopted with this woman and with the whole situation, but feared she was failing miserably in the face of Beverley's anguish.

'For…for being so kind,' said Beverley tremulously.

'Not at all,' Olivia replied. She wanted to say more, to say it was all part of the service or all in a day's work or something similar, but suddenly she found that she couldn't, that she was unable to speak for the lump that had risen in her throat.

In Theatre, she recalled that last conversation with Beverley and found herself wondering what Marcus would have made of the whole situation. And as she watched Nathan take his place and begin the operations that would ultimately save Drew's life, for the first time she allowed herself to wonder what would have happened if Marcus hadn't been killed. Would he have continued his secret affair with Beverley? Would she, Olivia, have found out? And if she had, would it have led to divorce? There were no answers to these questions, there was only the here and now and the way things were, and as she watched Nathan work and the soothing sound of a Mahler symphony filled the theatre, she knew it was time to put the past behind her. She found herself hoping against hope that Nathan felt the same way, that he too was ready to bury the past and all its painful memories and associations and be prepared to put his trust in a woman again. That she wanted that woman to be herself was becoming increasingly evident by the hour.

The operation progressed well without any mishaps, and when at last Nathan stood back to allow his assistant to take over, the first thing he did was to turn and seek out Olivia, indicating with one look and a slight raising of his eyebrows above his mask that all was well.

They left the theatre together and went to the relatives' room. Beverley was standing in front of the window and Matt was pacing up and down. They both froze as the door opened.

Beverley's gaze flew to Nathan's face. 'Is he all right?' she choked.

'He's fine,' said Nathan firmly. 'The operation went well, there were no complications and I've repaired the leaking valve.'

'Oh, thank you, Mr Carrington…' Beverley was obviously overcome with emotion. After Matt had shaken Nathan's hand and gone off to phone relatives with the news, Beverley said, 'Can I see him?'

'He's in Recovery at the moment,' Nathan replied, 'but they will soon be moving him into Intensive Care—you'll be able to see him then. You'll have to excuse me now, though. I'm due back in Theatre in a few minutes.'

An hour later Olivia escorted Beverley into HDU, where they found Drew sleeping peacefully, surrounded by monitors, tubes and drips.

Once again Beverly's tears got the better of her and this time, instead of brushing them away, she allowed them to stream unashamedly down her cheeks.

'He'll be fine now,' said Olivia gently, reaching out and re-assuringly touching Beverley's arm.

'I…I can't thank you all enough,' whispered Beverley.

'I'm going to leave you with Drew now,' said Olivia. 'I'll tell them at the desk to let Matt join you in a little while. I have to go and take a clinic…' With another squeeze of Beverley's arm she turned to go.

'Olivia,' said Beverley suddenly, and Olivia stopped. The woman's voice was low, urgent, and it was the first time she'd called Olivia by her first name and not Dr Gilbert.

'Yes?' Slowly she turned.

'There…there's something I want you to know,' Beverley said, and her voice faltered.

Olivia felt her stomach churn, wondering what on earth she could be about to hear now. That it was something crucial she had little doubt if Beverley's tone was anything to go by.

'It's about Marcus…Marcus and me,' she said.

'Actually,' said Olivia, 'I don't think I want to know any more…' It was the last thing she wanted, any details of their affair—she really didn't think she could bear that.

'This is different,' said Beverley. 'That night, the night he died—you thought he was on his way to see us when it happened, but it wasn't like that…'

'What?' Olivia stared at her.

'He'd already been to see us,' said Beverley.

Olivia turned away quickly. 'Look, I'm sorry but I really don't want to know anything about that…'

'No, listen, you don't understand—he'd come to tell me that he was going to tell you—'

'Please, Beverley, that's enough!' Olivia held up her hand but Beverley carried on talking as if she hadn't heard her.

'No, not about me—he was going to tell you about Drew.'

'But not about you! He was going to carry on keeping that a secret?' Olivia stared at her in astonishment.

'No.' Beverley shook her head. 'He wasn't going to tell you about me because…because there was nothing to tell.'

'What do you mean, there was nothing to tell? You told me you had resumed your relationship…'

'I lied,' said Beverley quietly.

'What?' For a moment Olivia couldn't take in what the other woman was saying. 'How could you lie about something like that?' she demanded at last.

'Because I wanted it to be true.' Beverley's voice was low now, so low that Olivia had to lean towards her in order to hear what she was saying. 'I wanted you to think that Marcus loved me when he died. It was wrong, I know it was…but he did love me once…and I…I still loved him.

When we met again and he started coming to see Drew, I wanted to start up the relationship again but…he wouldn't. He said he loved you.'

Olivia had been holding her breath and she let it go now, a long drawn-out breath, which could have been one of relief or of anger or a mixture of both.

'So on that dreadful night it was only Drew he'd been to see and it was then that he said he couldn't stand the secrecy any more and that he was going to tell you and hope that you would understand.'

As she finished speaking, both women instinctively turned and looked at the boy who lay before them. 'I had to tell you,' said Beverley at last. 'You have been so good to us—to both of us. You could have refused to treat Drew but you didn't, and I can never thank you enough for that, you and Mr Carrington, but…I couldn't go on letting you believe that about Marcus.'

'Well…' For the moment Olivia was speechless. 'Thank you for that,' she said at last. 'I wish I'd known before, it would have saved a lot of heartache. But I'm glad I know now.'

She wasn't quite sure how she got through the rest of that day because her thoughts were in utter turmoil, but somehow she did and after she'd taken her outpatient clinic and seen the last patient to the door, her phone rang.

'Olivia, it's Nathan,' he said, and at the sound of his voice she almost burst into tears.

'Oh, Nathan,' she managed to say at last.

'Olivia?' he said, 'What is it? What's wrong?'

'I've just had a talk with Beverley Jennings…'

'And she's upset you…'

'Well, no, not exactly…but I'd like to tell you about it when you have a minute.'

'What I was ringing for was to ask you if you would be prepared to take that chance we were talking about…'

'What chance?'

'On my cooking,' he said. 'I was going to ask you over for supper.'

'I would love to,' she said, and she knew the relief in her voice must have been apparent to him even down the phone. 'When did you have in mind?'

'How about tonight?' he said hopefully.

'Tonight would be wonderful,' she said simply.

'Where are you going, Mummy?' asked Charlotte.

'I'm going to supper with Mr Carrington.'

'Can we come?'

'No, darling, not this time,' said Olivia. 'This is a grown-up evening.'

'It's not fair.' Charlotte pouted. 'I want to see Jamie.'

'Jamie won't be there,' said Olivia. 'He's at home in Chester with his mum.'

'Mr Carrington said we'd be able to see Jamie again soon…'

'And hopefully you will.' Olivia had been sitting at her dressing-table, drying her hair, but she stood up now and looked down at her daughter, who had taken up a defiant stance, which was all too familiar to Olivia. 'Tell you what,' she went on quickly, 'if you come and help me choose something to wear, I'll come and read you an extra story before I go.'

'Lewis is asleep,' said Charlotte.

'Then it'll be just you,' Olivia replied. That seemed to please Charlotte, who scrambled up onto Olivia's bed and watched as she began taking clothes out of her wardrobe, rejecting some outright—'Oh, Mum, you can't wear that!'—putting others to one side as possible, then finally deciding together on a straight dress in a silky fabric with a layered hem, in soft blue and purple hues.

'That was the dress you wore to Auntie Claudia's party,' said Charlotte.

'Yes,' Olivia replied with a secret little smile, 'I know.'

'So, do you feel better now?' asked Nathan as he leaned across and refilled Olivia's wineglass. It was much later and the two of them were sitting together on the balcony outside his apartment. A light mist was beginning to settle over the Thames as the sun sank in the west, while the only sounds to be heard were from the various craft on the water below as they entered or left the docks.

'Yes,' she said slowly, 'I believe I do. I still feel that Marcus should have told me that he had a son, but now I've had time to think it all through I'm sure I will be able to find it easier to accept that his relationship with Beverley took place before he met me, rather than having to cope with the fact that he was having an affair at the time of his death.'

'What about Drew—is she going to tell him anything about this?'

'I'm not sure,' Olivia admitted. 'He seems happy and settled now—they both do now that they have Matt in their lives—but I think before Drew is discharged from St Benedict's I will say to Beverley that if ever there is a time in the future when he wants to know about his father's family, I shall be happy for her to tell him.'

'And what if he wants to meet Charlotte and Lewis?'

'Then we'll arrange a meeting.' She gave a little shrug.

'You know, Olivia,' he said, 'you really are the most incredible woman.'

'Don't be silly.' She tried to dismiss his remark but he, it seemed, had other ideas.

'No,' he said, 'I mean it. You gave money to this woman when you barely knew who she was—'

'That was for the boy,' she interrupted.

'Yes, I know, but you didn't have to do it. Then, when they turn up at the hospital, you take the boy's case when you could quite easily have passed the whole thing over to Hugh Jefferson—and now you're even saying if he wants he can meet and presumably form a relationship with your own two children.'

'They are his half-sister and -brother,' she protested mildly.

'Even so, I still think you are incredibly generous…'

'I care about children, Nathan, it's my job, it's what I do.'

'I know,' he said, 'and that's one of the things I love about you.'

'One of the…?' She turned her head and looked at him.

'Yep,' he said, and stood up. Leaning over her, he kissed the tip of her nose. 'You heard right, but it's only one of the things I love. I want to tell you about the others, but right at this moment if I don't rescue our supper we'll be eating burnt offerings.' With a chuckle he disappeared into the room behind them, leaving Olivia sitting on the balcony, sipping her wine and dreamily reflecting on what he had just said.

He'd set a table with a plain white cloth in front of the huge windows looking out across the Thames against the breathtaking backdrop of London at night. The only lighting in the room was from lightly scented candles, which he'd placed on every available surface, while in the background soft romantic music evoked memories and stirred her senses.

Supper was delicious—tender noisettes of lamb cooked in rosemary and served with fresh vegetables, followed by the lightest of soufflés served with raspberries and whipped cream.

'You gave me the impression I'd be taking a chance in trusting your culinary skills,' she said with a little sigh as she finished the last of her wine. 'That meal was just exquisite.'

'We aim to please.' He inclined his head slightly then, rising to his feet, he said, 'Let's go outside again.' Taking her hand, he led the way out onto the balcony where he slipped one arm around her shoulders and they stood together, admiring the scene—the lighted vessels as they skimmed the black satiny surface of the water, the myriad lights on the far bank, and above them, in the wide night sky, the stars that triumphed over all that man could offer.

'Are you happy?' he murmured after a while.

'Oh, yes,' Olivia replied. 'Happier than I've been in a long while.'

Then somehow she was in his arms and his mouth was urgently seeking hers, and this time there was no hesitation as she responded to his kiss. This time she simply gave herself up to the sheer pleasure of the feel of his arms around her, his lips on hers, his tongue gently seeking and exploring. If there were any slight warning bells trying to remind her that she still knew little about this man, that she could be setting herself up for another huge heartbreak, she swiftly dismissed them because for once she was only concerned with the moment and her own growing desire as her body reacted to his touch and began to ache for him.

And from there on it was only a matter of time before wordlessly he led her to his bedroom and carefully unfastened the zip of the dress she'd chosen to wear because she'd known, even on that very first meeting with him, that he had admired her in it. It fell into a pool of blue and lilac at her feet. Tenderly he removed the wisps of lace of her other garments then, after gently running his hands over her body, which caused her to gasp in delight, he lifted her into his arms and carried her to the bed.

He sat beside her on the edge of the bed and she watched as he discarded his own garments, admiring the lean lines of his naked back the short dark hair where it grew to a point at the nape of his neck and the muscles that rippled across his shoulders. It was a long time since she'd shared a man's bed. Would he find her attractive? She was, after all, the mother of two children. Just for a moment she felt a little stab of panic, but as he turned to her, stretched out beside her and began caressing her, she gradually relaxed and gave herself up to the sheer delight of being made love to.

'Olivia—you're beautiful,' he murmured, as her passion flared to match his own, and when finally the moment came and they became one, it felt so right that briefly, just before she surrendered to sweet oblivion, Olivia wondered how she could have ever doubted him.

CHAPTER TEN

THAT evening in Nathan's apartment had heralded the start of a heady period of getting to know one another, and as time went on and Olivia and Nathan found they had much in common, she knew she was falling in love with him. He took her out—to the theatre, to intimate dinners in unobtrusive restaurants and once to an open-air concert where they had listened, enthralled, to an exciting and moving performance. Sex between them was wonderful and for Olivia, at least, unexpectedly so as it involved a conscious feeling of letting go and learning to put her trust in another man again.

They spent time with the children, time she knew Nathan enjoyed, but she also knew he counted the days until Jamie could come down again. He went up to Chester one weekend, staying in a hotel, and although she missed him terribly, she was happy for him to spend some time with his son. On his return, however, he seemed unhappy about the situation he'd left behind.

'What was wrong?' she asked him gently.

'I'm not sure,' he replied. 'I can't quite put my finger on it. Susan was edgy and irritable, which I know from experience is not a good sign. Martin avoided me altogether, which is nothing really out of the ordinary.'

'And Jamie?'

'Jamie seemed OK,' he admitted.

'Well, that's the main thing,' she replied.

'Yes, I suppose so,' he said, but he still sounded less than sure, which left a tiny edge of apprehension in Olivia's mind over his relationship with his ex-wife.

At St Benedict's Drew's recovery was incident-free and at last the time came for him to go home. It proved to be an emotional moment for both Olivia and Beverley. Olivia had already spoken privately to Beverley and told her that if Drew wanted to know about his father and wanted to meet his half-brother and -sister, she was to contact her.

'I don't know how to thank you,' Beverley had whispered.

And then on the morning of his discharge, after the goodbyes she and Kirstin stood at the doors of the ward, watching as Beverley and Matt walked away down the corridor, each holding one of Drew's hands.

'D'you know something?' said Kirstin.

'No, but I'm sure you're going to tell me,' Olivia replied, bracing herself for what she might be about to hear. She didn't want to volunteer the information herself, saw no need for it now. If it came out in the future through Drew wanting to know, then so be it—but not now, for no reason at all.

'You're going to think this sounds really stupid,' Kirstin went on, oblivious to Olivia's thoughts.

'Try me,' she said bleakly.

'You know I said Drew reminded me of someone? Well, it came to me only this morning who it is—I think he looks like your Charlotte.'

'Charlotte?' said Olivia weakly. She'd been expecting Kirstin to say Marcus, not Charlotte.

'Yes, stupid, isn't it? But there was something about the expression in his eyes that reminded me of Charlotte.'

'Fancy that,' Olivia replied faintly.

Sara Middleton had also gone home, as had William Munns, their places taken by other children equally in need of the skill and expertise of the staff of Paediatrics.

Olivia herself was slowly getting over the revelations that Beverley had made. The relief she'd felt that Marcus had not been unfaithful to her since their marriage had been overwhelming, even though it had taken her some time to try to understand why he had felt the need to keep Drew's existence a secret from her. In the end, she could only reach the conclusion that his need for secrecy had been all bound up in his childhood and adolescence, when his parents had forced him to end his relationship with Beverley and the difficulty and embarrassment he would have been forced to face if it had subsequently come out, all of which would have been so at odds with the face he displayed to the world as that of a highly successful barrister.

And as time passed and she grew closer to Nathan, she at last began to hope that it really was time to put the past behind her and get on with her life. Until one day when the order of their lives, like the coloured pieces in a kaleidoscope, were shaken once again and fell into an unexpected pattern.

She and Nathan had slipped into a routine of cooking supper for each other fairly frequently, and once again it was Olivia's turn to go to his apartment but that particular Friday afternoon, as she was clearing her desk before the weekend, Nathan came to her consulting room. She noticed immediately that he looked troubled.

'What is it?' she said quickly, as he came right into the room and shut the door behind him. 'What's wrong?'

'I'm not sure,' he said, running one hand through his hair in a distracted fashion, 'but I'm afraid I'll have to cancel this evening, Olivia.'

'Oh,' she said with a sharp stab of disappointment. 'What's happened?'

'I need to go up to Chester,' he said. 'I'm so sorry. But Susan has just phoned me—she says she and Martin have split up.'

'What?' Olivia stared at him, realising that her initial feeling of disappointment had given way to something else— a sinking feeling that she wasn't immediately able to define. 'Do you know why?'

'No.' He shrugged. 'She didn't really say. She was a bit hysterical on the phone but she wants me to take Jamie until things are sorted out. I have to go,' he went on.

'Of course you do.'

'I don't want him in the middle of all that, especially if things get ugly. I am sorry, Olivia—you do understand, don't you?' He looked at her pleadingly.

'Yes,' she said, 'of course I do. You must go, Nathan, there's no question about that.'

And she meant it, she really did. She knew she would have been the same if it had been Charlotte or Lewis in the same situation.

So if that was the case, why did she feel so dreadful after he had gone, so lonely and so insecure in spite of the fact that he'd taken her in his arms right there in her consulting room, kissed her and told her that he loved her and that he'd be back soon?

It was because of Susan. Deep down she knew that, just as she knew that she'd never quite accepted the fact that Nathan had really got over his divorce or even that he had never quite stopped loving Susan.

So had she been deluding herself all along? Had he quite simply been waiting for this day, knowing that eventually it would come, that his ex-wife would wake up to the fact that it was really him she'd loved all along and beg him to return?

All along she'd harboured a slight misgiving where Susan was concerned. There hadn't really been anything tangible, apart from at the beginning when Nathan had said he didn't think he'd ever marry again—but, then, hadn't she too said the same thing?—and that he wasn't sure he'd be able to trust a woman again after Susan's betrayal. Susan had hurt him badly, Olivia knew that. In preferring Martin to him, she'd wounded his male pride. How would he react now, with her saying she'd left Martin? Would he feel vindicated, quietly triumphant? Secure in the certain knowledge that it had been him she'd wanted all along?

And hadn't she felt the same way when she'd thought Marcus had betrayed her and had eventually found that he hadn't—the sweet relief from that had overwhelmed her? The difference between her and Nathan, however, was that Marcus was dead and their story was ended, but Susan was very much alive and their story presumably could be resumed. A sudden wave of desolation swept over her and she pressed her hand against her mouth to prevent a sob escaping. Had she simply been a fool into rushing into a relationship with Nathan?

Nathan settled into his seat and switched on the CD player in preparation for the long drive north. He'd hated having to leave Olivia, especially when he'd seen the disappointment in her eyes, a disappointment that had matched his own. But really he'd felt he had little option other than to go to be with Jamie at this time, which would be so unsettling for the boy, especially as he'd been through it all once before. Susan had been practically incoherent on the phone, flinging wild accusations at Martin and in the end demanding that Nathan come and take Jamie until things were sorted out. Susan, he knew from bitter experience, could be totally unpredictable and, really, there was no way of knowing quite what he would find on his arrival.

The one thing he did know, however, the one thing of which he was completely certain, was the way he felt about Olivia. Since meeting her and being with her, she had brought a dimension to his life he had never dreamt of.

Helene met Olivia in the hall when she arrived home from work. 'You are early,' she said.

'Yes,' Olivia agreed wearily, 'I'm early.' Then, not wanting to discuss events any further, she said, 'Is everything all right?'

'Yes, the children are playing in the garden. Mrs Lathwell-Foxe phoned. I say you phone her back.'

'Very well, Helene, thank you.'

She didn't want to speak to Claudia, didn't want to speak to anyone really, but at least it was something to do—anything to take her mind off what might happen when Nathan reached Chester. So, much later, after the children were in bed, she went into the sitting room, and as she sat down and dialled Claudia's number Oscar came up to her and rested his head on her lap.

'Olivia? Oh, I didn't expect you to ring tonight.' Claudia sounded surprised. 'Helene said you would be having supper with Nathan. All I wanted was to ask you both over for dinner next weekend.' She paused. 'Aren't you going to Nathan's this evening?' she added curiously.

'No, Claudia, not this evening,' she said.

'Oh?' Claudia sounded surprised. 'I hope you two haven't rowed or anything.'

'No, Claudia, we haven't rowed…' Olivia trailed off, uncertain how to explain exactly what had happened.

'So what is it? What's wrong?' Claudia demanded. When Olivia still found it difficult to continue, she went on, 'Honestly, you and Nathan seem to be getting on so well…'

'Yes, we are…' Olivia replied haltingly.

'So what on earth has happened? Something has happened, I can tell by your voice.'

'Susan happened,' Olivia replied, as she did so absentmindedly stroking Oscar's head.

'Susan? What? As in ex-wife Susan?'

'Yes.'

'What on earth does she have to do with anything?' The astonishment was obvious in Claudia's voice.

'She phoned Nathan at work today.'

'What did she want?'

'I'm not sure exactly. She told him she and Martin have parted…and she wanted him to go up to Chester.'

'For heaven's sake! I hope he told her where to go.' Claudia paused. 'He did, didn't he?' she added incredulously.

'Not really…'

'You're not telling me he's gone!' Claudia exclaimed.

'Yes, but…he's gone because of Jamie,' she added quickly, as if by saying it she could convince not only Claudia but also herself. 'Susan apparently wanted him to take Jamie until things are sorted out.'

'Oh,' said Claudia, 'that's different.' She paused then said in a much softer, gentler voice, 'You're not worried about this, are you, Livvy?'

'I'm not sure…'

'You needn't be,' said Claudia emphatically. 'Nathan is crazy about you—anyone can see that. And there's no way on this earth that he'd have Susan back again, if that's what you're worried about. Is that what's worrying you?' she demanded.

'Yes… No… Oh, Claudia, I don't know,' she said helplessly. 'You know I wasn't at all sure I was ready to move on after Marcus but then…finding Nathan, well, it's been wonderful and has shown me that I can love again. I guess I can't quite believe it's for real.'

'Oh, it's for real all right,' said Claudia firmly. 'Just you wait and see. And there's no way Nathan would have Susan back. According to Rory, she treated him abominably so just you stop worrying.'

'Well, we'll see,' said Olivia. Suddenly she felt overwhelmingly weary.

'Now, you get a good night's sleep,' said Claudia, 'and things will look much better in the morning.'

If only she could believe that, Olivia thought as she said goodbye to her friend and hung up.

She really did recognise Nathan's desperate need to see his son. She would be exactly the same if it were Charlotte or Lewis in the same situation. But somehow she couldn't get the picture out of her head of Nathan travelling through the night to be with his son and his ex-wife. Anything could happen from here on in, she was only too aware of that. Claudia had been emphatic that Nathan would never take Susan back, that he would be wary of her doing the same thing to him all over again. And maybe that was so. But Claudia had overlooked the one thing that could swing things in Susan's favour, and that was the love they both felt for their son. Jamie could be the one factor that just might persuade Nathan to reconsider reconciliation.

The possibility of that stayed with Olivia throughout that long night as sleep eluded her and she tossed and turned in an agony of uncertainty.

Saturday was a strange day, with Olivia feeling as if she was suspended in limbo. There had been no word from Nathan and while she longed to hear from him, at the same time she dreaded what he might tell her. In the morning she took Charlotte to her dance class and Lewis to the pool for his swimming lesson. After she'd collected both children they returned to the house for lunch. 'Were there any messages?' she asked Helene.

'No.' Helene shook her head. 'Mr Carrington has not called.'

'That wasn't what I asked,' said Olivia.

'I know,' Helene said sympathetically, and hurried off to the kitchen.

They carried their lunch through to the garden and sat around the table beneath the rose-covered wooden pergola. It was another hot day, slightly oppressive and without as much as a breath of wind, and as they ate the food that Helene had prepared—cheese, ham, salad and crusty bread— Oscar came out of the house and padded around until he found a patch of shade where he flopped down to rest, panting noisily.

After lunch they lolled around for a while, reading books and magazines, then later, when it was a little cooler, the children took themselves off to the end of the garden and played in the tree-house that Marcus had built for them in the lower branches of a large lime tree. Olivia, tired from her sleepless night, sat on the comfortable garden swing-chair and drifted dreamily for a while.

Nathan was there in her dream, she could hear his voice, he'd called her name—she knew she should rouse herself really and go indoors to face the hundred and one weekend tasks that awaited her, but she was reluctant to do so because if she did, her dream would disappear and he would be gone again.

'Olivia.' It was so real, so close this time she was forced to open her eyes.

Nathan stood before her, Jamie by his side. He really had called her name, it wasn't a dream. 'Nathan!' She sat upright. 'How on earth did you get back so quickly? And, Jamie—how lovely to see you again.'

'I'll tell you all about it,' he said. 'Where are the children?'

'They're playing in the tree-house. Jamie, why don't you go down and surprise them?'

'All right,' Jamie said, and with a quick glance at his father, who gave him a reassuring nod, he made his way down the garden. If there'd been any doubt about the warmth of his welcome, it was quickly dispelled by the shrieks of delight from Charlotte and Lewis.

'They'll be over the moon,' said Olivia, as Nathan sat beside her on the garden seat. 'They've been on about Jamie coming to visit ever since the last time he was here.'

'It's only a flying visit, I'm afraid,' said Nathan. 'He has to be back for school on Monday, but under the circumstances I thought it was important that he spend a bit of time with me.'

'So what exactly are the circumstances?' Olivia threw him an apprehensive glance, then listened carefully as he went on to explain what had happened on his arrival in Chester.

'I talked to Susan at length,' he said. 'She told me the reason that she and Martin have parted is because Martin's firm want him to relocate to London.'

'Is that so terrible?' said Olivia. 'A lot of us do live in London.'

'I know,' Nathan replied dryly, 'that's what I told her, but she'd got herself in a state about leaving her friends and her parents and her life in Chester. Anyway, one thing led to another and she and Martin had huge rows. When I pointed out that presumably it would be just as difficult for Martin to relocate, with his family being in Chester, it hadn't seemed to occur to her. Likewise for Jamie leaving his friends and his school and his grandparents but, then, most things always are about Susan and her needs.'

'So how were things when you left?' asked Olivia.

'Well, I'd only been there for an hour or so when her parents arrived and between us I think we made Susan think that this move needn't be the end of the world—that they needn't even move right into London, that there are lots of nice places within easy striking distance of both London and Chester. Anyway, Jamie and I stayed the night with Susan's parents—I've always stayed on good terms with them so there was no problem with that.'

'And Martin, where is he?' asked Olivia curiously.

'He's here in London apparently. Jamie's going to go back to Chester with him tomorrow afternoon. By the time we left, between us we'd managed to persuade Susan to phone Martin. She then spoke to her mother this morning and I gather from her that she and Martin have talked at length.'

'So you don't think she meant it when she says they've parted?'

'No, I don't,' he replied. 'That was just Susan being Susan. But it did sound like they were going to consider the suggestion of living somewhere between Chester and London.'

'If they did that, it would be easier for you and Jamie to see each other,' said Olivia.

'Don't you think I'd already worked that out?' said Nathan with a smile.

Olivia was silent for a moment then, throwing Nathan a sidelong glance, she took a deep breath and prepared to say what she knew had to be said. 'Did Susan think there was a chance that you and she might get back together again?' she said at last.

He threw her a startled glance. 'I wouldn't have thought so,' he replied, 'not for one moment. Susan knows that our relationship, our marriage, was well and truly over a very long time ago—she also knows she needs to work at her relationship with Martin, otherwise that will go the same way.' He paused and looked at Olivia. 'You didn't think that was what was going to happen, did you?' he asked gently.

'I wasn't sure what to think,' she admitted. 'I know you were deeply upset when Susan left you because you told me so, then you said she'd left Martin and I also knew that you have always been concerned about the effect the break-up had on Jamie.'

'So you thought I might have been prepared to try to patch things up?' he said quietly.

'Like I say, I didn't know what to think.' She shrugged.

'There would have been no point,' he said. 'Even if that had been what Susan wanted, and she didn't, it would have been simply that—a patch-up. It would never have worked and Jamie would have been the one to suffer in the long run when it all fell apart again. And besides, there's another greater reason for knowing it would never have worked.' As he spoke, he reached out and took her hand.

'And what is that?' she whispered.

'Because I'm in love with you,' he said simply. 'I told Susan about you,' he added.

'Did you? What did you say?'

'I told her that I'd met you since coming to London, that I'd fallen in love with you and that I want to spend the rest of my life with you.'

Olivia felt her pulse quicken at his words. 'Nathan…' she said at last. 'You told me once you doubted you'd be able to trust a woman again.'

'Olivia,' he said, 'I would trust you with my life.' He paused and, searching her face hungrily, said, 'But what about you? Are you ready to put your trust in anyone again?'

'Not just in anyone,' she said softly, 'only in you.' She heard his breath catch in his throat then without a word he leaned across and covered her lips with his own.

'What do you think,' he said, drawing away after a long moment, 'the chances would be of you coming over to my place tomorrow night so that we could have the supper we missed on Friday night? Do you think Helene would oblige again so soon?'

'Oh, I have no doubt she would…' she replied. They were silent for a while, watching Oscar as he gave little yelps in his dream. 'He's dreaming he's a puppy again and can still chase rabbits,' she said with a smile.

'How do you think your children will react to this?' Nathan asked a little later.

'Me and you?' Olivia raised her eyebrows. 'I would say they'd be delighted.'

'And I know Jamie will,' said Nathan with a sigh.

'So, really, Mr Carrington, there isn't anything to stop us, is there?'

'No, Dr Gilbert,' he replied, taking her face between his hands and gazing deeply into her eyes, 'I don't believe there is.'

'Shall we call them and tell them now?' she said softly.

'Yes, let's,' he said, 'but first, I want another kiss.'

MILLS & BOON®

Live the emotion

_Medical
romance™

THE CHRISTMAS MARRIAGE RESCUE
by Sarah Morgan

When her marriage to gorgeous Spanish consultant
Alessandro Garcia hit the rocks, Christy left. Now
the children want to spend Christmas with their
father! Christy returns with them and is roped into
working in Alessandro's A&E department. Could
this be their opportunity to mend their marriage…?

THEIR CHRISTMAS DREAM COME TRUE
by Kate Hardy

When Kit and Natalie Rogers lost their baby,
nothing could ever be the same again. Six years
later they reunite as colleagues in the paediatrics
department at St Joseph's. They rediscover the
intense feelings they once shared and both start to
wonder if their secret wish to be together might just
come true.

A MOTHER IN THE MAKING *by Emily Forbes*

Free spirit Dr Tilly Watson takes up a job at her
local hospital, working closely with her charismatic
new boss, the gorgeous Dr Jock Kelly. Tilly cannot
ignore the fact that she is falling for Jock. But
although he seems so settled, and their lives are
destined to take different paths, Tilly can't help but
wonder if maybe, just maybe, they might have a
future together.

On sale 3rd November 2006

Available at WHSmith, Tesco, ASDA, Borders, Eason,
Sainsbury's and most bookshops
www.millsandboon.co.uk

MILLS & BOON®

1006/03b

Live the emotion

Medical romance™

THE DOCTOR'S CHRISTMAS PROPOSAL
by Laura Iding

It's Christmas at Trinity Medical Centre, and nurse Dana Whitney loves the festive season. If only she could get her boss into the Christmas swing! For Mitch, Christmas only brings up painful reminders. Yet there's something about Dana that inspires him. Can he find the courage to love again?

HER MIRACLE BABY *by Fiona Lowe*

Surviving a plane crash in the forests of Australia sparks the beginning of a real connection between Dr Will Cameron and Nurse Meg Watson. Meg knows she has no future with Will – he wants what she is unable to give him – children. But after sharing a passionate night together, a miracle happens…

THE DOCTOR'S LONGED-FOR BRIDE
by Judy Campbell

It was not until Dr Francesca Lovatt announced her engagement that Jack Herrick realised that he had always loved her. Unable to bear seeing her with another man, he left town. But when he returns as registrar at Denniston Vale Infirmary he finds that Francesca is still single! This time round things will be different.

On sale 3rd November 2006

Available at WHSmith, Tesco, ASDA, Borders, Eason, Sainsbury's and most bookshops

www.millsandboon.co.uk

researching the cure

The facts you need to know:

- Breast cancer is the commonest form of cancer in the United Kingdom. **One woman in nine** will develop the disease during her lifetime.

- Each year around **41,000** women and approximately **300** men are diagnosed with breast cancer and around **13,000** women and **90** men will die from the disease.

- 80% of all breast cancers occur in post-menopausal women and approximately 8,200 pre-menopausal women are diagnosed with the disease each year.

- However, survival rates are improving, with on average 77.5% of women diagnosed between 1996 and 1999 still alive five years later, compared to 72.8% for women diagnosed between 1991 and 1996.

Breast Cancer Campaign is the only charity that specialises in funding independent breast cancer research throughout the UK. It aims to find the cure for breast cancer by funding research which looks at improving diagnosis and treatment of breast cancer, better understanding how it develops and ultimately either curing the disease or preventing it.

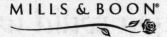

MILLS & BOON®

BCC/AD 2006 b

During the month of October Harlequin Mills & Boon will donate 10p from the sale of every Modern Romance™ series book to help Breast Cancer Campaign continue *researching the cure.*

Statistics cannot describe the impact of the disease on the lives of those who are affected by it and on their families and friends.

Do your part to help, visit
<u>www.breastcancercampaign.org</u>
and make a donation today.

researching the cure

All you could want for Christmas!

Meet handsome and seductive men under the mistletoe, escape to the world of Regency romance or simply relax by the fire with a heartwarming tale by one of our bestselling authors. These special stories will fill your holiday with Christmas sparkle!

On sale 6th October 2006

On sale 20th October 2006

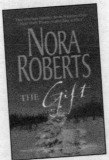

4 FREE

BOOKS AND A SURPRISE GIFT!

We would like to take this opportunity to thank you for reading this Mills & Boon® book by offering you the chance to take FOUR more specially selected titles from the Medical Romance™ series absolutely FREE! We're also making this offer to introduce you to the benefits of the Mills & Boon® Reader Service™—

- ★ **FREE home delivery**
- ★ **FREE gifts and competitions**
- ★ **FREE monthly Newsletter**
- ★ **Exclusive Reader Service offers**
- ★ **Books available before they're in the shops**

Accepting these FREE books and gift places you under no obligation to buy, you may cancel at any time, even after receiving your free shipment. Simply complete your details below and return the entire page to the address below. You don't even need a stamp!

YES! Please send me 4 free Medical Romance books and a surprise gift. I understand that unless you hear from me, I will receive 6 superb new titles every month for just £2.80 each, postage and packing free. I am under no obligation to purchase any books and may cancel my subscription at any time. The free books and gift will be mine to keep in any case.

M6ZED

Ms/Mrs/Miss/Mr ....Initials ....

BLOCK CAPITALS PLEASE

Surname ....

Address ....

....

....Postcode..................................

Send this whole page to:
UK: FREEPOST CN8I, Croydon, CR9 3WZ